MW00581755

This page is intentionaly left blank.

I Never Danced with My Father

By
Sherry J. McFarland

BASE Publishing, LLC

I Never Danced With My Father

All counseling advice depicted in this novel was strictly written for fictional purposes only. If you require counseling please seek a trained, qualified professional. Likewise, if suffering from domestic abuse please contact the National Domestic Abuse Hotline or a local agency in your area.

National Domestic Abuse Hotline: 1-800-799-7233

Printed in the United States of America
ISBN 13: 978-0-9828539-1-7 | ISBN 10: 0-9828539-1-2
225 Pkwy 575 | Unit #2591
Canton, GA, USA | 30188

Email: authorsherryjmcfarland@gmail.com

Daddy,

You may be gone but you will never be forgotten. You are one of the greatest fathers I know. A man of honor, integrity, humility, strength, compassion and love. You will always be my hero and I will always love you.

In loving memory of

Raymond Edward James

- THE WOUNDS OF AN INJURED HEART CAN LAST A LIFETIME -

Contents

CHAPTER 1

Felicia

Denial In The Face Of Truth

DYSTHYMIA *[dis-thahy-mee-uh] - Persistent depression lasting up to*

two years or more; despondency or a tendancy to be despondent.

Hovering somewhere in the realm between consciousness and unconsciousness, Felicia finally managed to open her eyes long enough to bring the swirled pattern of the ceiling into focus. She wasn't sure if she had actually blacked out or if she had simply closed her eyes for a few minutes. She scanned the room trying to gather her bearings and figure out where she was. The sound of dripping water and the last rays of daylight shining through those cheap thrift store curtains hanging at the window solemnly reminded her that she was in her kitchen.

How could she forget those curtains? They had been hanging at her kitchen window for ten years. The flowers that ran along the bottom edge of them were now a dull, muted, dingy shade of yellow. They had never been exactly as bright and vibrant as she had wanted them to be even when she first bought them but the sun had definitely taken its toll on them after all these years making them look even worse.

Felicia stared at the curtains, as if seeing them for the very first time, until she became keenly aware of how much she really hated them. Hate wasn't the right word; she despised them. She always had but she had never admitted to herself why until today. She hated them because they were hand-me-downs. In fact, practically everything they owned had been either been given to them, picked up from a yard sale, or purchased from a second-hand store. Looking at them now she realized that those curtains were a bitter reminder of just how miserable her life had become.

Felicia attempted to sit up which proved to be a huge mistake. She grimaced as a sharp pain shot through her head. She knew It was only her imagination but somehow the sound of the dripping water seemed to intensify the pain. It was too much to bear and instantly, she   regretted the decision she had made to try and move.

For the moment, the cold linoleum of the kitchen floor was her refuge. As long as she lied perfectly still the intensity of the pain was not as severe. Somehow she found solace there because the coolness and immobility that the floor provided were comforting to her. She softly rubbed her hands back and forth across the linoleum as she lied there in agony; praying for God to strip the pain from her body. Given the choice to die at that very moment she might have chosen death but she knew she could never leave her kids. She could never give up on life because her children were the only things she had left in this world worth living for.

Felicia garnered enough strength to turn over onto her stomach. She maneuvered her body inch by inch across the floor using only her forearms, until she finally reached the cabinets on the other side of the kitchen. Like a soldier crawling on the ground in combat she somehow managed to drag the entire weight of her body across the kitchen floor. But by the time she reached the other side, the room felt as if it was spinning all around her. She was consumed with a sensation that reminded her of a cartoon character that had been bonked on the head with a ring of stars swirling around its head.

Fighting through the pain she reached for the handle on the refrigerator door for leverage which allowed her to pull herself upright into a seated position on the floor. She closed her eyes for a few minutes with her back firmly resting against the cabinet doors. She was halfway there but she knew the hardest part was yet to come. Felicia was determined to stand to her feet so, with her eyes still closed, she rolled over on all fours and balanced herself on her hands and knees. She gripped the sink for extra support and with all her strength she pulled herself up off of the floor.

"Oh my God", she whispered out loud. Her head was swooning and for a brief moment she thought she was going to be sick. She slumped over the kitchen sink and waited until the wave of nausea subsided. The aching in her body felt worse than any pain she had ever experienced before in her entire life; other than perhaps the pain of giving birth. Her body felt like she had been hit by a train but she had done it. With God's help and for the love of her children she was able to stand up!

This wasn't the first time Marcus had kicked Felicia with his steeled-toe work boots but she couldn't remember ever hurting this badly before. To make matters worse, she was supposed to be at work in an hour but she knew from the pain in her side that she wouldn't be able to work tonight. It felt like her ribs were broken. Instinct was telling her that she needed to go to the hospital to make sure, but she dreaded having to go because she didn't know how she would ever be able to explain what had happened to her and make her explanation believable.

Each and every time Marcus had hit her in the past she would always tell herself afterwards that it was going to be the last time.

She would convince herself that she was not going to let him beat her anymore. She said it the last time, and the time before that, and the time before that. In fact, Felicia had said it so many times before that she wasn't even sure if she believed it herself anymore.

Of course he had apologized for beating her; just like he always did. Telling her how sorry he was and how much he loved her. He would swear to Felicia that it was never going to happen again. Then in the very next breath he would invalidate his apology by having the audacity to blame her; telling her that it was her own fault for making him so angry in the first place. His reaction was that of a typical physical abuser - shift the blame from yourself onto your victim.

Over the years Felicia had managed to recognize most of the warning signs and subtle nuances that indicated Marcus's temper was about to spiral out of control. She always tried to do everything within her power to circumvent the triggers that might spark his anger. But no matter how hard she tried there were times when she just wasn't successful at diffusing his temper and preventing his anger from culminating into violent outbursts. In fact, keeping Marcus's rage dormant had become a daunting task. It was like trying to extinguish a forest fire with only one cup of water at a time.

Even though his rampages were occurring less frequently, they were becoming more and more violent. In fact, Felicia honestly couldn't even remember what had provoked his anger this time. Not that it really mattered, because whatever it was, nothing could have warranted the intensity of the beating he had just inflicted on her. She was just grateful that he had never taken out his anger on their children.

The left side of her face was throbbing with pain. Felicia sensed that her right eye was swollen nearly shut because she had no peripheral vision on her right side. She faintly tasted the traces of blood in the corner of her bottom lip and she could barely move her jaw back and forth. However, the fact that she had some amount of movement was a good sign that her jaw had not been broken.

Marcus's laughter resonated from the living room where he was watching the television; oblivious to what he had just done.

Felicia didn't care where Marcus was, she was just grateful that her kids were in their bedrooms and couldn't see her like this. She knew they had heard her and Marcus fighting but at least they had not actually witnessed the beating. Instinctively they always knew to stay in their rooms whenever they heard their parents fighting.

As much as they loved their father they also feared him. Felicia tried to shield them as much as she could from the ugly truth about their father and his random fits of rage. She didn't do it for Marcus's sake; she did it to protect her children's innocence and view of the "real" world. She explained to them that all grownups fight sometimes and reassured them that they did not need to worry because "daddy would never hurt mommy". It was a lie but that was the only way she knew how to keep her children from intervening in the middle of one of their fights and possibly getting hurt. They were kids but they were growing up fast. She didn't know how much longer she was going to be able to hide the truth from them.

In fact, their son DeMarcus was ten now and he was becoming more and more aware of what was really going on between his parents. Felicia knew it bothered him because of the questions he would always ask her after they had been fighting. Her greatest fear was that, sooner or later, DeMarcus was going to try to defend her by jumping into the middle of it. Marcus had never hit the kids before but she didn't know how he would react if DeMarcus actually tried to fight him or questioned his authority. She just prayed it would never come to that.

As Felicia began to make her way out of the kitchen, she was relieved to discover that she could actually breathe a little bit better now that she was standing. She still had to take shallow breaths but the pain was beginning to ease off slightly. Taking very small steps, she walked out of the kitchen and into the hallway. She was only able to take a few steps at a time before she would have to stop and rest, but at least she was making progress. Marcus happened to look up from the television and saw Felicia standing in the hallway slightly slumped over, resting her weight on the wall.

"What the hell is wrong with you?" Marcus asked. Unfortunately, Felicia didn't answer fast enough to Marcus' liking, so he shouted, "DID YOU HEAR ME and why are you walking so damn slow?"

Marcus took a good look at her and it finally registered to him how badly he had hurt her. For the first time Felicia actually saw fear in Marcus's eyes when she turned around to answer him. However, that look of fear only lasted a fleeting moment as he quickly became agitated again. He walked towards her cursing and immediately began blaming her for making him so angry in the first place. He even had the nerve to tell her she brought all of this on herself.

Felicia recoiled from Marcus's touch when he reached out and tried to examine her swollen face. As she pulled away from him the swerving motion caused her to lose her balance. Marcus reached out and grabbed her in an effort to prevent her from falling back into the wall. He put his arm around her waist to help steady her until she could regain her balance.

As she stood there grimacing in pain from the touch of his arm around her waist, he lifted her shirt and swore under his breath when he saw the dark bruises that had formed over her rib cage.

"You might have some broken ribs. Does it hurt when you breathe?"

"Yes, it hurts if I try to breathe," Felicia answered. "I have to take short, shallow breaths."

"You need to go to the hospital," he replied, standing there looking at her incredulously, as if it were her fault that she needed medical attention.

"I'm sorry," Felicia mumbled an apology.

"You should be. Now you won't be able to go to work and we'll probably be up all night sitting in the emergency room," he replied, clearly annoyed with the prospect of having to wait up all night in a hospital emergency room. "Just go wait in the living room while I get the kids ready," he ordered her.

"No! Please don't," she pleaded with Marcus as she reached out and grabbed his arm in an attempt to prevent him from going down the hall to get the kids. The sudden movement caused her to swoon and Marcus reached out once again; catching her to prevent her from toppling over.

"I-I can drive myself to the hospital. You can stay here with the kids. There's no sense in you and the kids wasting time sitting around the hospital for hours waiting with me," Felicia urged, hoping he would see the logic in her reasoning. "Unless you have a life threatening injury you know how long it can take sometimes to be seen by a doctor."

"Do you think I'm gonna let you go to the hospital all alone so you can tell them that your husband did this to you?" he hissed.

"I won't tell them what happened, I promise. Please Marcus!" she implored. "I don't want my kids to see me like this. I won't tell anyone what happened. I won't!"

Eying her suspiciously, Marcus finally relented but not before pointing his finger in her face and threatening her by saying, "You hear me and you hear me good! You better NOT tell anyone what really happened, if you know what's good for you!"

"I won't," she replied, relieved that he wasn't going with her but she was more relieved that her children wouldn't have to see her like this.

"Well, let me help you down the hallway", he offered.

"That's ok; I'm fine. I can make it by myself".

"You don't look fine".

"I am. I just have to take my time".

"All right then, suit yourself. At least I offered to help you."

With that being said, Marcus went back into the living room and started watching TV again. Leaning against the walls to support her weight, Felicia made her way down the hallway. It amazed her how such a tiny little house suddenly appeared to be so expansive in size when it seemed to take forever to finally reach her bedroom.

Recalling Marcus's reaction at seeing her injuries she was a little apprehensive about turning on the bathroom light. She had to brace herself when she finally saw her reflection in the mirror. She wasn't prepared for the image that was staring back at her. Felicia's face was severely bruised and swollen. She looked like she had just finished going ten rounds in a heavy weight boxing match with Muhammed Ali; and lost.

She barely recognized the person staring back at her in the mirror. Her face was so numb that she could only faintly feel the warmth of her tears as they trickled down her face. She was thankful for the rich, cocoa brown complexion of her skin. Her darker skin tone reduced the visibility of the bruises and the black eye that would have been more evident had her skin tone been even one shade lighter.

How in the world had she let herself become this poor, helpless shell of a woman? She was trapped in a world of violence that she didn't know how to escape from. The harsh and brutal reality of what her life had become only caused her to cry more. She was a prisoner with no way out. Felicia's reaction was that of a typical physically abused victim – guilt, shame, hopelessness and low self-esteem.

CHAPTER 2

Naomi

Femme Fatale

Naomi tugged at the hem of her skirt to remove any creases and finished fastening the buttons on her blouse. Mr. Larosa was using the mirror located in his private bathroom to straighten his tie. The custom designed lavatory was located in Mr. Larosa's office behind a mahogany door which ran along the wall. It was situated just to the right of a huge wet bar. When the door was closed, it blended in very discreetly with the décor of the office. It took a discerning eye to distinguish the door from the rest of the wall; just as it had been designed to do. Naomi stepped in front of the mirror and kissed Mr. Larosa one last time before trading places with him. She needed to freshen up before the client for his one o'clock appointment arrived.

Her initial meeting with Mr. Larosa was unlike any she had ever experienced before. On the day of her interview she was astonished to find that he had actually memorized her entire resume. He knew so much about her; she was certain he must have had her investigated because he knew things about her that clearly were not on her resume. In fact, the interview felt more like a one-sided conversation with Mr. Larosa doing most of the talking. He concluded the interview by telling Naomi how impressed he was with her but if the truth be told it was Naomi who was impressed with him. She later learned that Mr. Larosa researched anyone that he conducted business with. He taught her to always size up your competition in advance; little did he know that was a strategy that she already knew all too well.

Naomi had worked for Mr. Larosa for almost three years now and they had been having an affair for….almost three years now. They both knew where this relationship was headed the moment he offered her the position as his Executive Assistant. Naomi had done her research on Mr. Larosa and his company. Although she had no doubts in her ability to land the position, she decided to up the ante a little bit --just in case the decision came down to her and another candidate. She didn't want to leave anything to chance so she wore what she liked to call her "killer", "go get em", business suit. This suit pushed the boundaries and failed to meet the criteria of an appropriate business suit which is exactly what she planned. The skirt was an inch too short, a half size too small, and the jacket was on the borderline of showing way too much cleavage to be business appropriate. But it did the trick; she landed the position.

Mr. Larosa may have had his reasons for hiring her but on a professional level she worked hard and she was damned good at what she did. No matter what happened between them, work always came first for Naomi and she took her job very seriously. Work was work. The affair, on the other hand, was just a bonus with fringe benefits. Mr. Larosa took good care of her, so likewise, she took good care of him. They were both adults and they had a mutual agreement that benefited them both with no strings attached. Just the way Naomi liked it.

Mr. Larosa's one o'clock appointment arrived ten minutes early for the meeting. His name was Lance Davenport. According to the client dossier Lance's family owned a large transportation company of which Lance was the former President. Currently he was the owner of three restaurant franchises, his own signature restaurant, and other various business ventures. He was also tall, dark, handsome and very wealthy. With Mr. Larosa's advice, Lance Davenport stood to gain significant investment returns that could prove to be very lucrative. Naomi always did her homework when it came to business, finances or personal matters. Not to mention, working for one of the nation's top real estate and private investment brokers didn't hurt either.

Even though she knew Mr. Larosa was ready for his meeting she deliberately waited a few more minutes before announcing the arrival of his client. That was another tactical business strategy that Mr. Larosa had taught her: make a business client wait just a few minutes whenever they wanted something from you. It gives you the upper hand. However, Naomi also had personal reasons for making this client wait; the delay gave her more time to survey Mr. Lance Davenport. His name sounded so elegant and regal as she rehearsed the sound of his name over and over again in her head. Lance Davenport definitely had her full attention and she wanted to get to know him on a first name basis.

She tapped on the door before sticking her head into Mr. Larosa's office to inform him that his client was waiting. He was pulling out the papers that he had stuffed inside of the top drawer of his desk. They made eye contact and smiled at each other; both of them unmistakably amused by the memory of what had just transpired on that very desk less than twenty minutes ago.

"Mr. Larosa will see you now Naomi announced as she opened the door, ushering Lance Davenport inside. She gently closed the door behind her but not before stealing another admiring glance at Lance. "My, my, my, he looks just as good from behind," she thought to herself. She could tell that the suit he was wearing had been tailor made. You couldn't find a suit off of any store rack that would fit the muscular and athletic physique of his body like that. Lance was six feet four inches tall, and two hundred and five pounds of lean muscle mass. His skin was velvety smooth and he wore an immaculately trimmed goatee. Lance could very easily have been mistaken for a runway model or a Hollywood action superhero.

Instinctively Naomi looked down at Lance's left ring finger observing the absence of a wedding band. Not only was she astute when it came to business but she was also just as astute when it came to fashion and men. She generally preferred married men, however, in the case of Mr. Lance Davenport she might have to make an exception. Naomi shied away from single men because all too often they became clingy and demanding. Those were characteristics she abhorred in a man. They want to know where you are, what you're doing, who you are with, when you will be home and the list goes on and on. As far as Naomi was concerned; No thank you! She would take a married man over a single man any day of the week.

In her opinion married men had too many other obligations and commitments to try to keep tabs on her and that suited her just fine. She was not looking for any kind of committed relationship which is why she preferred married men over single ones. For Naomi, being single gave her the freedom from having to worry about what to cook for dinner, helping the kids finish their homework, washing dishes, washing tons of laundry or any of the other stresses associated with domesticated "wifely" chores.

Sure, she started out like most little girls: with the grandeur of finding a husband and growing up to get married but that notion ended a very long time ago. Love always led to a broken heart and as far as Naomi was concerned love was a waste of time. Instead, she dated married men because it allowed her to experience all the pleasurable benefits of being a wife without the commitment; besides there was always an extra apology gift for those holidays and occasions when they had to be with their family and not her. To Naomi, the advantages of dating married men far outweighed the disadvantages.

When the meeting was over Lance emerged from Mr. Larosa's office appearing even more jovial than he had been when he first arrived.

"Mr. Larosa asked me to check with you about scheduling my next appointment," he replied standing in front of Naomi's desk.

She knew Mr. Larosa would have taken care of that task himself and would never have asked a client to make his own appointment. Besides, this appointment had already been set up weeks ago on a monthly recurring basis. Lance's request seemed contrived to her but she decided to play along.

"Your next appointment is already scheduled for next month Lan…I mean Mr. Davenport. Every third Tuesday of the month at one o'clock PM," Naomi informed him, wondering why he needed to schedule an appointment that he knew was already scheduled on a recurring basis.

"I need to change next month's appointment. I will be out of the country the week of our scheduled meeting so I need to inquire if Mr. Larosa has any time available to meet the following week."

Naomi checked Mr. Larosa's calendar. "I'm sorry but he doesn't have anything available that week," she replied.

"That's fine. I appreciate your checking for me. Why don't you take my business card and call me if anything changes. Otherwise, I will just see Mr. Larosa during our regularly scheduled meeting the following month."

Lance presented Naomi with his business card. As she extended her hand to retrieve the card from him, he grabbed her fingers and pulled them toward his lips. He simultaneously slipped the card into her fingers and kissed the back of her hand. That was definitely a smooth move and he had just earned himself a few brownie points with her.

She turned the card over after Lance had left the office and noticed that he had written a date, a time, a location and a phone number on the back of the card. Was this his gallant way of asking her out on a date, yet relinquishing full control? He was apparently sparing her from the discomfort and awkwardness of turning him down if she wasn't interested in going out with him.

Lance was definitely a refined man and just that quickly he had earned himself additional brownie points. If Naomi played her cards right things could prove to be very interesting so she elected to definitely break her rule about dating single men. She just prayed that Mr. Lance Davenport would not disappoint her and cause her to change her mind.

CHAPTER 3

Susan

The Secrets That Find Us

PARANOIA *[par-uh-noi-uh] - An unfounded or exaggerated distrust of others*

sometimes reaching delusional proportions.

Susan and Larry answered the phone at the same time. The man's voice on the other end of the line sounded a little unusual as he asked to speak with Larry. He sounded unsure of himself. Susan could hear the nervousness in his voice.

She ascertained from the brief conversation she overheard that her husband did not seem to know the man on the other end of the phone so she honestly didn't think much of it. She just assumed it was someone her husband had worked with in the past or maybe a former classmate. After all, it's not uncommon to forget the sound of someone's voice you haven't heard in a very long time. She even thought maybe the man was trying to sell something. Knowing her husband could do a better job of getting rid of a solicitor without committing to anything she hung up the phone and let Larry deal with the call.

It wasn't until Larry walked into the den a few minutes later that she became concerned. She knew something was wrong. Susan had never seen Larry look at her that way in the entire twenty years they had been married. Something was very wrong. Even though he was looking at her it was as if he were looking through her. His eyes appeared glazed over.

He sat down next to her on the couch but didn't say anything at first. He just sat there motionless. Larry was staring aimlessly into space as if he were in a trance. He was scaring her but she waited until he finally said something and when he did, she could not believe what her husband told her. Surely, she had misunderstood what Larry said. This had to be some kind of joke except he wasn't laughing.

A son? How in the world could Larry have a son? When? Why hadn't he ever told me about his son? How could he do this to me? How could he lie to me all these years hiding his son?

Susan felt as if she had been tackled by a line-backer and had the wind knocked out of her. Thank goodness she was already sitting down because she didn't think her legs would have been strong enough to support her.

A million questions were racing through her mind but the most important question was; was this really true? She glanced over at Larry searching for answers. He didn't have a guilty look on his face like she thought he would and he wasn't pleading for her forgiveness. Instead he appeared to be just as shocked and confused as she was.

Larry said that he had no idea that he had a son. He wasn't even sure yet if it was really true. The young man on the phone was twenty two years old and his name was Larry Julian Baker, but everyone called him Julian. Susan breathed a small sigh of relief when she mentally did the math in her head and realized that Larry had not been unfaithful to her during their marriage. His son had been born before they were married but that still did not explain why Larry had never told her about Julian. Although he wasn't a Jr., he had been named after Larry, taking his first and middle names.

None of this was making any sense to Susan. Her husband was totally devoted to their two children. So, regardless of his responsibilities, Larry would never have knowingly skipped out on his child. Family meant too much to him. He could never abandon his children so she had to believe that he did not know about Julian.

How could some woman have had my husband's child and not tell him after all these years? Why did she tell her son and not Larry? What was the status of their relationship at the time that she was pregnant that he would not have known that she was carrying his child? Had it been a casual relationship; a one night stand? Had this woman lied to her son all these years by pretending that my husband was his father and now he had called her bluff? Was she ashamed of her son's real father and why would she name Larry of all people? All of these thoughts were racing through Susan's mind.

Larry's father had walked out on his family when Larry was a baby. He had left his wife all alone to raise three kids by herself. He just left for work one Friday morning and never came back. But, despite his father leaving, Larry made the best of his circumstances and made a good life for himself. His brother and sister hadn't faired so well; always blaming someone else for their problems and thinking that the world owed them something. Larry had never really missed what he never had and he vowed that he would always be there to take care of his kids. That's why none of this made any sense to Susan; it was too much out of character for her husband.

Larry was the most loving father Susan had ever known. She always teased him that he overindulged their kids for what he missed out on as a child. She knew he loved their kids and he meant well so most of the time she let him spoil them. Their kids were good kids. Larry and Susan had made sure that they taught their kids to appreciate and value everything that they were given. They knew what it meant to work hard for what you have and to save for a rainy day. Susan couldn't have asked for a better husband or a better father for her children.

"Baby, are you ok?" Susan reached over to Larry and wrapped her arms around his waist hugging him reassuringly.

"I'm ok, I'm just in shock. Baby I had NO idea I had a son."

"I know. I can only imagine what you must be feeling right now. Why didn't she tell you?"

"I honestly don't know. I met her in Houston right before I left to go to graduate school. Before I met you"

"It just doesn't make any sense to me. I mean why didn't she tell you she was pregnant?

"Baby I don't know."

"Do you think she's telling the truth?"

"I honestly don't know. I mean it's possible. We did sleep together.

"You didn't use protection!"

"Baby, please calm down. Yes, we used protection."

"Well maybe she's lying."

"I don't know and if she is lying why would she wait until now after all these years? I don't think she's lying."

Susan felt a sour churning in the pit of her stomach when Larry acknowledged that he didn't think that Julian's mother was lying; when she, on the other hand, was so sure that this woman was. She had to be lying. That was the only explanation that Susan could rationalize in her mind at the moment.

"Well how…"

"Susan, you're asking me questions that I don't have the answers to."

"I'm sorry. I didn't mean to badger you. I just have a lot of questions."

"I know you do baby," Larry replied reassuringly as he reached out and covered Susan's hand with his own. "I have a lot of questions too, but I didn't want to make Julian feel like I was interrogating him. This is between me and his mother. By the way, he gave me her number. I didn't ask him for it, he just gave it to me. I hope you don't mind."

"No, I don't mind. I know you have questions and the only way we, I mean you, are going to get to the bottom of this is by contacting her. Can I ask you one last question?"

"Yes Susan," Larry sighed.

"What's her name?"

"Vanessa. Her name is Vanessa Baker."

Susan left Larry alone and went upstairs to get ready for bed. She knew Larry wasn't a virgin before they met but she also knew he wasn't cavalier when it came to sex either. She knew she had no right to judge anyone but part of her had to wonder what kind of woman could just readily sleep with someone they barely knew. There had to be more to their relationship because Susan just couldn't imagine Larry casually having sex with someone he barely knew either.

As Susan approached their son Devin's door she noticed that it was closed but she could still hear his music playing softly as she got closer. The Kids! She hadn't even thought about them. What were they going to tell the kids? "Guess what guys you have a brother!"

Did Larry's son even want to have a relationship with him? She presumed he did, otherwise, he probably would not have reached out and contacted Larry in the first place. How would Julian react when he learned he had a brother or sister, assuming he didn't have other siblings already?

Susan knocked on Devin's door before sticking her head in to say goodnight. Just as she expected Devin was sitting at his desk listening to music while he did his homework. She found it quite amazing sometimes how children pick up some of their parent's traits. She used to enjoy listening to music too while she did her homework. She had to have soft music playing in the background or else she would find herself being distracted by the sheer quietness.

Devin was 16 and a sophomore, honor roll student in high school. He loved music, playing the guitar, and sports. Devin's personality was very similar to Susan's. He was honest, trustworthy, dependable and loyal to a fault but if you ever crossed him you could consider yourself having lost a devoted friend forever.

Devin inherited his athletic abilities from Larry. In fact, he made the varsity basketball team his freshmen year which is very rare. Devin started out practicing on the Junior Varsity team, however, when his coach saw his skills in practice he introduced him to the Varsity coach. The Varsity coach invited Devin to practice with the team and by the time the season opener began Devin was on the roster.

Devin walked over to the door and gave his mother a kiss after she informed him that she was going to bed a little early. She reminded him not to stay up too late after he finished his homework. He was responsible and Susan knew that he would go to bed when he was supposed to but she felt that every now and then you have to remind your children of things they already know; it lets them know that you love them and you care.

When she checked in on Danielle she found her sprawled out on her bed wrapped in a blanket reading a book. Danielle had inherited her love of reading from Susan. Like her brother, she was an honor roll student as well. Danielle was equally a daddy's girl just as much as she was a mama's girl. Although, now that she was twelve it seemed as if she was beginning to drift more towards being a mama's girl. Danielle reminded her mother that she needed to purchase some supplies for an upcoming project before Susan left her room and kissed her goodnight.

Although Devin and Danielle were definitely old enough to know what was going on Susan wasn't ready to tell them anything just yet. Not until she and Larry had more answers. Since that wasn't about to happen tonight she closed the door and decided to go to bed and try to get some sleep.

A couple of hours later Susan felt the bed shift from Larry's weight as he climbed into bed beside her. Occasionally, if Larry found his wife already asleep when he came to bed he would wrap his arms around her and snuggle up close to her, but not tonight. Tonight he got in the bed and turned his back towards Susan. She knew that he wasn't ready to talk about it yet and she wanted to give him his space. He had a lot on his mind. They both did but whenever the time came that he was ready to talk she would be there to listen.

Susan closed her eyes even though she wasn't really asleep. Normally she would have turned over or said something to let him know she was still awake but she decided not to say anything tonight. Considering the current circumstances she thought that it might be best to leave things unsaid.

Susan lay awake almost half the night listening to Larry breathing. She had never distrusted her husband before and she didn't like the way she was feeling right now. She wished she could relax and fall asleep but she spent the rest of the night trying to make rhyme or reason of this situation in her head. As much as she tried to ignore it something just didn't add up. Somebody was lying; they had to be. But for now she made the decision to trust her husband.

CHAPTER 4

Kandi

Incomplete

Kandi awakened to the sounds of birds chirping outside her bedroom window. She didn't need to set an alarm clock because they were there to greet her every morning like clockwork. Their melodious chirping was reminiscent of some kind of roll call. They would beckon one after the other as if to let the world know that they were present and accounted for. Some people might find them annoying but she welcomed them. It reminded her of the simple things of life; before the day began and everything became hectic.

Kandi rolled over and found Trent still sound asleep. On most mornings Trent would have already risen out of bed before her. This was a rare occasion so she slipped out of bed and tiptoed across the floor, being extra careful to avoid the spot in the wooden floor that creaked so she wouldn't wake Trent. She gently opened the drawers of the dresser and retrieved her under garments.

She jumped in the shower and decided to forgo washing her hair this morning. She was in a hurry and didn't have time to properly style her hair once it was wet. While waiting for the water in the shower to warm up she picked out her clothes and shoes from the walk-in closet.

To Kandi's astonishment Trent was still asleep when she stepped out of the bathroom. To save more time, she decided to put her makeup on at the office. Smiling mischievously she closed the bedroom door and headed downstairs to grab her breakfast and lunch she had prepared the night before. So far so good! She had managed to sneak out of the bedroom without awakening Trent.

"Good Morning", Trent replied, startling Kandi as he stood in the threshold between the kitchen and the living room.

"I thought you were still asleep", Kandi replied.

"I was. I didn't hear you get up this morning so I came downstairs to see if you were still here. You must have been really quiet".

"I was. I didn't want to wake you", she offered, trying to be as casual as possible; hoping Trent wouldn't realize that she had been purposely trying to avoid him.

"Why didn't you wake me up", he asked?

"I thought maybe you wanted to sleep a little while longer. Besides, I have an early meeting this morning and I don't want to be late."

"Are you sure that's all it is?"

"Of course that's all, what else would it be?"

"How about you are deliberately trying to avoid me?"

"Please tell me we are NOT going to have this conversation again," Kandi sighed, closing her eyes and shaking her head.

"Yes Kandi, we ARE going to have this conversation again."

"Trent, if I don't leave now I'm going to be late for my meeting. I promise we will talk about it tonight after dinner."

"No, Kandi. You promised we were going to talk about this the last time I tried to have this conversation with you. It's starting to be the same thing over and over again. Every time I try to talk to you about this you're either too tired, you're going to be late, or whatever other excuse you can come up with to avoid having this conversation."

"Babe, I know. I know, and I promise you we will talk about it tonight for sure. I promise. Ok babe?" Kandi replied imploringly, like a little child begging for a drink of water as a last attempt to delay going to bed.

"Ok Kandi," Trent relented, throwing his hands up in surrender. We will wait and talk about it tonight, but no more excuses. I mean it."

Secretly she had just won this round. However, in an attempt to call a truce and render a smile from Trent she evoked the best "puppy dog face" she could and kissed him on the cheek before grabbing her briefcase and walking out the door for her meeting. Once again Kandi had eluded the conversation but somehow she didn't feel confident that she was going to be so lucky tonight. In fact, they had discussed this topic so many times before that she had actually lost count. Unfortunately, they never seemed to be able to reach any sort of resolution because inevitably one of them would walk away out of sheer frustration; promising one another that they'd discuss it later.

Trent was a very patient man but sometimes Kandi sensed that he was getting very close to the end of his rope. In all honestly, she didn't know how much more he could take. On the other hand, she didn't know how much more she could take either and that scared her. She truly loved him and she really was not trying to push him away. Deep down inside she knew what he wanted but she just couldn't give it to him right now.

One of the things she loved about Trent was the fact that she never had to be something she was not in order to earn his love. He loved her unconditionally for who she was. Kandi loved Trent with all her heart and she knew that he loved her. So of course she wanted to get married; someday. Marriage just didn't fit into her life plans right now. She simply needed a little more time.

Kandi had been mapping out her goals and dreams ever since she was ten years old and so far everything in her life had occurred in order, according to her plans. Marriage was on her agenda right after she made Senior Partner but first she needed to make Junior Partner with the firm and that wouldn't occur for another year or two. Once she made Senior Partner she and Trent would get married the following year. From the very beginning of their relationship Trent had known about her goals and aspirations so it wasn't as if she was springing a surprise on him. She just didn't know why he was being so persistent now.

Trent and Kandi met back when they were in law school together. There weren't that many African Americans in their law program to begin with and although they did not intentionally conspire to get placed in the same study group, they ended up in the same group none the less. They had a lot in common so it was only natural that they later found themselves drawn to each other.

They moved in together about a year after they graduated from law school and passed the bar. Now, after almost six years of dating, Trent was ready to get married and Kandi was not; thus the dilemma of this perpetual conversation they could never seem to finish. Trent was the ideal man and she knew he would make an excellent husband. There was no doubt in her mind about that. It's true that people throw the term around loosely but Trent truly was her "soul mate". Sometimes she felt as if God had read her mind and designed Trent especially for her.

When asked by the professor on the first day of their Civil Procedure Law class to introduce themselves Kandi gave her ten year goals while everyone else in the class gave their five year goals. Trent knew Kandi's plans since the day they met. In fact, he told her countless times before that her drive and determination were among some of the qualities he admired the most about her. He teased her all the time that she had the tenacity of a bull; when she set her mind to something there was no stopping her. Everything was happening according to her plan. That's why she was so confused by his urgency to get married.

She graduated at the top of her class and accepted a position with Schuster & Weitzman law firm upon graduation. Mr. Schuster, a senior partner with the firm, was her mentor and had taken her under his wing. They had won some big cases together and now she was being groomed for a position as a junior partner with the firm. She would be a fool to give all that up now.

Kandi's plan was to make junior partner, continue working with Mr. Schuster and then make senior partner after he retired; then she would be ready to get married. Another three years after they were married they would be ready to start a family. She would be thirty-five years old which in her opinion was the perfect age to start a family. She and Trent would both be well established in their careers, financially stable, and they would have had over ten years together with just the two of them.

Her plans couldn't be any more perfect. Furthermore, they were practically living together so she just didn't see the need to rush and get married. It's not like they were never going to get married. They would get married one day but she refused to let anything or anyone stop her from achieving her goals. Not even Trent who was the love of her life.

As much as she would like to resolve this issue and put it behind them she was not looking forward to having this conversation tonight. Regrettably, one of them was not going to be happy with the outcome and she didn't know if their relationship could survive another impasse.

CHAPTER 5

Melina

The Comfort We Find In Each Other

Melina had never changed the overall design and layout of her office the entire five years she had occupied this space. Everything was basically in the exact same place as it had been the day she moved in. This was so out of character for her because she thrived on change. It was her belief that keeping things the same or staying in one place too long can make a person become stagnant. Change makes us examine ourselves which can be a good thing. Change forces us to reinvent ourselves and propels us into action. On the other hand, sometimes fear to embrace the unknown can prevent us from changing and moving forward. Fear can cause us to stay in one place too long. Change may not always produce a tangible action but at least it causes us to think and that IS action.

Melina was always redecorating her home so she really had no viable explanation as to why she had not done the same here in her office. Maybe it was because she had countless unfinished projects at home on her never ending "to do" list and had never gotten around to creating one for the office. But she had a reason to remodel it now.

She had already met with a general contractor a few months ago to review her ideas and now all of the structural work had finally been completed a couple of days ago. She was in her office surfing the internet looking for a few additional accent pieces to complete her new office renovation while she waited for a delivery. Her office had been previously designed for one on one and small family counseling. Across from her desk had been a single chair that she sat in during counseling sessions. Adjacent to the single chair was a small L-shaped sectional sofa. She suddenly had a brainstorm to capture the images for her scrapbook of what her office used to look like because all of that was about to change. She wished she had thought of taking pictures before the structural changes had begun but at least she could capture the before and after decoration photos.

The new vision for her office was an environment that offered complete relaxation. She wanted something spa-like and refreshing; yet very homey to present a cozy and warm atmosphere. Something very laid back and casual that would instantly make a person feel at ease. Her desire was to create an ambiance reminiscent of a group of friends simply gathering together to talk.

The new layout involved moving her desk along the left side wall as you entered the office. The sofas and chairs were being delivered that afternoon and would be placed in front of the huge wall of windows where her desk currently resided. Melina wanted the new cozy seating arrangement to be the focal point when you entered her office. She had the old sofa recovered and the plan was to move it into the outer office reception area. The contractor had built a partial L-shaped retaining wall that would conceal her "official" office area and her desk would be relocated behind it. She had already purchased some artificial plants and a piece of artwork to cover the wall.

The renovation was a complete makeover with the exception of the wall on the left side of the office. That wall was currently flanked with built in book cases which were being incorporated into the new design behind her new desk area. On the right hand wall were a set of smaller, three feet high, wall to wall matching built in bookcases. She had already purchased a new Kuerig hot beverage machine to place on top of the shorter bookshelves along with aromatherapy oils and candles to accentuate the décor. She classified her new design as bohemian spa beach resort meets warm cozy mountain retreat.

Melina considered herself to be one of the lucky people in this world who are fortunate enough to have a career doing what they really love. For her, that love was helping others. Even as a child she had a passion for helping people. She was the neighborhood negotiator growing up. As a teenager, she was the go to person that all of her friends confided in. Many times she was the voice of reason who could talk them out of doing something crazy. She believed one of the main reasons they came to her was because she could be trusted to keep their secrets. The other reason was her compassion.

Against the advice of her parents and her high school guidance counselor Melina went to college and declared Psychology for her major. They thought that she was more academically suited for Computer Science or Engineering. In their opinion she was "wasting her time" on a lesser degree. They even warned her that without an advanced degree she wouldn't be able to find a job in Psychology when she graduated; but that was exactly her intention. Her plan was to continue her education and pursue her doctorate degree. So, she stayed in college until she received her PhD. and then went into private practice for herself. Her practice has been growing for almost fifteen years now which has allowed her to have such a powerful impact on people's lives.

She listens to people without passing judgment so they feel comfortable talking to her. They work as a team. She serves as the coach and together she works with her clients through life issues to find resolutions for their problems. She allows them to be whoever they are with no pretenses. That's what she loves most about her job.

About two years ago Melina founded a non-profit organization for young teen girls called "H.O.P.E. (Helping Others Prevail Emotionally)" where she serves as the Executive Director and Staff Counselor. She started this organization as part of her Pro Bono work. It was sort of her way of paying it forward because her heart had always been partial to young women and there are far too many of them growing up with so much pain. They are hurting and have no idea how to heal from their pain. If they don't learn how to heal their pain many of them will carry that pain with them to adulthood and some of them will carry it for the rest of their lives.

People think that once you become an adult you get over your hurt but the truth is most people don't. That was the main reason why Melina had also recently decided to expand her pro bono services to adult women. She had actually stumbled across a post on an internet site several months ago that really intrigued her, thus fueling her desire to organize a women's therapy group.

The online article featured a fifty year old woman who had recently found out who her real father was after he died. She had thought all her life that if she could just find out who her father was she would be able to put all of the hurt behind her but she found out she was wrong. The man who was her father had lived on the same street that she had grown up on all her life. She wondered how many times she had waved at this man. Had he known all along that she was his daughter? She was convinced that he knew because he never waved at the other kids in the neighborhood, only her. She hated him for it now because it was "so unfair" she had been quoted as saying. He had the liberty of watching her grow up knowing that she was his daughter but she had not been afforded the same opportunity to know who her father was because now he was dead.

She was still hurting and she had every right to be. Melina knew that there was a need to help women just like the woman in the article but she did not have the capacity to take on any more clients. So, she established this women's support group as another extension of her pro bono work and now here she was remodeling her office and taking on yet another project.

The subject of Fatherless children had always been near and dear to Melina's heart for a very long time. In fact, she wrote her graduate thesis on the effects of growing up without a father in the household. During her research she talked to so many children and it broke her heart to hear the pain in their voices and to see the hurt on their faces. That is why she devoted her life's work to helping young girls raise their self-esteem, to teaching them how to become positive role models and to encouraging them to pursue college.

Melina met Kandi about fifteen months ago when she became a volunteer with H.O.P.E. and as they got to know each other better Kandi confided in her about the issues she was having with her boyfriend. Kandi was the first person that Melina asked to join the women's support group. Melina sensed that Kandi's problems were deeper than just her reluctance to get married. She knew that Kandi too had grown up without her father and Melina was certain that was the root cause of her true issue. Melina wanted to help her so that was where the brain child to start a woman's support group was birthed; through Kandi.

Kandi had a friend who she felt could benefit from a support group like this and asked Melina if she could invite her and just like that the women's support group had two initial participants. The plan was to meet with the women one night a week in Melina's office. Now all she needed to do was put the finishing touches on the redecorating and everything would be ready for their first meeting.

CHAPTER 6

Felicia

Fear Is The Norm

Norm *[nawrm] - The unwritten but understood rules of a society or culture for the behaviors that are considered acceptable and expected.*

In the past four years Felicia had never missed a day of work so her boss was very understanding when she called and informed him she wouldn't be able to come to work that evening. She apologized for the short notice and lied a little bit by telling him that she had been in a minor accident which prevented her from performing any strenuous activities. She was a good worker and she was very reliable so she hoped that her reputation would be enough for her boss to believe her.

He told Felicia not to worry; that he would take care of things. He reassured her that everything would be alright and he would cover her shift until she was able to return to work. In fact, he insisted that she take all the time she needed and to take care of herself. He just requested that she check in with him every day to let him know how she was progressing along. That was why she always went to work on time and always did her best because you never know when you might need a favor.

Now that work was taken care of she wasted no time in grabbing her purse and keys off the kitchen table before Marcus changed his mind about letting her drive to the hospital alone. Her rib cage still hurt so she decided against wearing a seatbelt. She didn't want to do anything to aggravate the injury any further so she resolved that she would just have to take her chances against being pulled over by a cop for not wearing a seatbelt. Although she still couldn't take a deep breath, she was relieved that she was finally able to breathe without winching.

Felicia pulled into a parking space on the side of the hospital near the emergency room entrance. She grabbed her shades and jacket before getting out of the car. She knew she looked crazy but she didn't want anyone to see her disfigured face. She decided that the best way to cover it up was by wearing her shades and pulling the hood of her jacket over her head. Now she totally understood how celebrities must feel when they were trying to avoid being seen by the paparazzi.

About thirty minutes after signing in with the patient intake attendant Felicia was astonished to hear her name being called over the hospital PA system. This had to be an all-time record; to be seen so soon after arriving to the emergency room. Under normal circumstances your name would never be called this quickly unless you were bleeding, in acute pain or suffering from chest pains. She wasn't suffering from any of these conditions but she decided she wasn't going to look a gift horse in the mouth.

She was instructed to undress down to her under clothes and put on the hospital gown. It hurt like hell when she tried to raise her arms over her head to remove her shirt. She didn't want to attract anyone's attention so she covered her mouth with her hands and clenched her teeth in an effort to suppress the urge to scream out loud. She sat on the edge of the bed and tried to think of another game plan to remove her shirt without causing too much pain.

Instead of reaching overhead this time she gently eased one of her arms downward, out of the sleeve of the shirt she was wearing. Repeating the same process she removed her other arm. She tilted her head slightly forward and was able to gently finish removing her shirt without lifting her arms up above her head. Eventually, she managed to finish undressing before the nurse arrived to check her vital signs. After answering several rudimentary questions, Felicia laid back in the bed and closed her eyes. The hospital bed felt so good that all she wanted to do was close her eyes and fall asleep forever.

She wasn't quite sure how long she had been lying there but somewhere in the distance she could hear someone calling her name. She slowly opened her eyes and saw a doctor standing beside the bed. At first she was perplexed but comprehension set in and she remembered that she was in the emergency room of the hospital.

"Hi. Mrs. Riley, I am Dr. Anderson," she replied, extending her hand towards Felicia.

Dr. Anderson began her examination by poking and prodding Felicia in various places as if she were a specimen in some type of science experiment. Dr. Anderson was pleasant enough and tried to make small talk in light of the current situation. She asked Felicia the typical question as she examined and touched different areas of her face and body; "does this hurt"? Felicia thought to herself, "so far, so good"; until the doctor started asking the questions that Felicia knew she would eventually ask her. As much as Felicia tried to deny it there was no way to avoid the inevitable.

"From the looks of things you appear pretty banged up. Mrs. Riley can you tell me how you sustained these injuries?"

Felicia told her that she had fallen down the stairs at home. What Felicia failed to tell her was that her house was a single story home. Dr. Anderson rubbed her forehead and made a small sigh.

I NEVER DANCED WITH MY FATHER | 47

Felicia got the sense that the doctor didn't believe her and her words confirmed Felicia's suspicions.

"Ma'am, I hope that you can appreciate that I have seen many different types of injuries and your injuries are not indicative of someone who has fallen down the stairs. I'm sorry but a person generally would not obtain these types of injuries from simply falling down a flight of stairs. Likewise, there are also injuries that are not present on your body that should be there and would indicate a fall as you have described. Mrs. Riley your injuries display evidence that would suggest someone had been beaten or perhaps involved in an automobile accident at best," she informed Felicia.

"I fell down the stairs. I was coming downstairs when my bedroom shoe came off and it caused me to slip and lose my balance," Felecia tried to explain.

"How did you fall when you lost your balance?"

"I-I don't know. It all happened so fast," Felicia replied, trying not to raise her voice. Dr. Anderson was making Felicia nervous with her questions.

"Mrs. Riley, are you afraid of something or someone?"

"No, I am not afraid of anything. I told you I fell down the stairs." Felicia's voice had clearly raised a decibel or two and although Dr. Anderson was smiling, Felicia could tell that she was still skeptical about her version of what had happened to cause her injuries.

"You don't have to be afraid to tell me the truth. We can get you some protection and we can find you a place to stay where you won't have to worry about being safe."

"Look, Dr. Anderson, I understand your concern but I am telling you the truth. I fell down the stairs," Felicia replied as convincingly as she could. "That's all that happened. End of story."

Felicia was relieved when Dr. Anderson finally backed down and didn't pursue the issue any further. Her tone changed and she became patronizing. She wasn't buying Felicia's story but she left the examination room to go write up the discharge papers while Felicia got dressed. When she returned she reviewed the instructions on the paper with Felicia. She asked Felicia one last time if she had any questions. Felicia had no further questions so she signed the release forms.

Felicia smiled at Dr. Anderson and graciously accepted the papers that the doctor had given her. Dr. Anderson wanted to say more but she refrained. They simply eyed each other with a knowing glance and smiled slightly. Whatever it was Dr. Anderson was about to say she let it go. They had reached a nonverbal truce.

Just as Felicia was about to leave the examining area, a pamphlet fell on the floor from the stack of papers Dr. Anderson had given her. When she picked it up she noticed that the pamphlet had information about a women's support group. Felicia was astonished when she turned the brochure over and read the back of it. The name printed on the back in bold letters read "Dr. Melina Bradshaw". She recognized the address too because she had worked there for the past four years. She had seen the name plenty of times outside the door leading to suite 350. All this time Felicia had no idea Dr. Melina Bradshaw was that kind of doctor. It made sense now. That's what all those extra letters that were printed behind her name meant.

Within the stack of papers she also discovered a flyer for battered women. Anguish gripped Felicia and her heart began to quicken. Her hands were trembling as a shiver ran up her spine causing her to drop the entire stack of papers. There in front of her lay a simple piece of paper that had the power to change her life forever but she felt paralyzed to pick it up. Fear held her captive and every second that she hesitated, she allowed reality to creep in to remind her that she could not keep this flyer. The last thing she needed was for Marcus to find it. He would never believe that she hadn't said anything to anyone. She had to get rid of the flyer but she didn't want Dr. Anderson to think that she was unappreciative of her help so Felicia waited until she had gotten outside the hospital before she threw the pamphlet and flyer in the trash can.

Just as he always did, Marcus went on about his regular routine as if nothing had ever happened. He hadn't even bothered to wait up for Felicia to get home from the hospital. Instead she had found him in bed fast asleep. She had come to learn the best thing for her to do was to move on and try to get things back to normal as best she could.

Normal for Felicia meant doing everything she had to do to prevent this from happening again. It meant going out of her way to make sure that everything at home ran according to Marcus's specifications which entailed dinner being ready before he got home from work. His first order of business was to take a shower as soon as he walked through the front door. She would pick up his sweaty and grimy clothes off the floor, put them in the dirty clothes hamper and have a fresh change of clothes waiting for him the moment he stepped out of the shower. Equally as important was her routine to have an ice cold beer waiting for him in the fridge to go along with his dinner.

Felicia and the kids would sit at the table and wait for Marcus to join them for dinner. No one could eat until Marcus sat down at the table. After he blessed the food she would fix his plate, the kid's plates and then her own. At least he honored the family value of eating dinner together. He was so pleasant with the kids; asking them about their day, laughing with them about something funny that may have occurred at school. The kids brought out the good side of him. But it was like living with Dr. Jekyll and Mr. Hyde. As soon as dinner was over Marcus would retreat to the living room to watch TV and that was the end of family time.

Felicia and the kids would clear the dishes off the kitchen table. She allowed them to finish the rest of their homework in the kitchen while she washed the dishes and packed lunches for the next day. After their homework was finished she would make sure that the girls were bathed and dressed in their pajamas so that they would be ready for bed when bedtime arrived.

Their son DeMarcus had long outgrown the need for anyone to give him a bath so most of the time he and Felicia would just talk before it was time for her to leave for work. DeMarcus was very mature for his age and very observant. He didn't say anything but she could see it in his face and she really didn't like the way he was looking at his father when he thought no one was watching him. As much as he loved Marcus, Felicia suspected from some of their conversations that he was slowly loosing respect for his father and that could only mean trouble.

She always tried her best to make light of the situation between Marcus and her by encouraging DeMarcus not to worry about it. She reiterated to her son as often as she could that everything would be alright but she knew he was starting to doubt her. He wanted to protect his mom but it wasn't his job to protect her; it was her job to protect him. The best way Felicia knew how to protect her children was to encourage them to do their best in school so that they could have a better life than she did. She wanted them to have a chance in life. She always kissed DeMarcus and the girls good bye before she left to go to work and reminded them how much she loved them. Day in and day out, year after year, this was her normal.

Felicia wasn't fully healed but that did not stop her from calling her supervisor that morning to let him know that she was coming back to work that night. He thought it was a little too soon but she assured him she was up to it. She was eager to get back to work so that she could have her solace again away from Marcus and the sooner the better.

She saw the lights still on in Dr. Melina Bradshaw's office which could only mean she must be working late. Dr. Bradshaw was usually gone by the time Felicia got to work but for the past few weeks Felicia had found her still in her office working when she got there to clean the suite. Her office was currently being remodeled so Felicia had a little more to clean than normal. The workers were pretty good about cleaning up after themselves but there always seemed to be an extra amount of dust everywhere after they had been working.

Felicia didn't want to disturb Dr. Bradshaw so she said hello and went on about her work. She didn't realize Dr. Bradshaw was watching her until she looked up and saw Dr. Bradshaw standing beside her.

I NEVER DANCED WITH MY FATHER | 51

"Here let me get that for you," Dr. Bradshaw offered to empty her own trash can.

She had grabbed the trash can out of Felicia's hands before she could protest so Felicia simply said, "Thank you."

"Are you ok", she asked Felicia?

"Yes, I'm fine."

"I was just asking because I haven't seen you in several days", she replied, smiling at Felicia as she always did?

"Oh, I didn't think you would notice?"

"Of course I noticed. I saw Mr. Jordan last week cleaning the building and he forgot to restock the coffee pods which I know you always do. Thank you by the way."

"You're welcome and you don't have to thank me. I don't mind," Felicia replied.

"Well I want to thank you anyway and let you know how much I really appreciate it. I also want to apologize for the extra mess that's being made while my office is being remodeled."

"It's fine. It's really not that big of deal and it doesn't take that much more time or effort for me. It's just a little extra dusting every day. That's all"

"So, were you on vacation?" she asked Felicia.

"No, I wasn't on vacation. I had a minor accident."

"Oh, is that how you got your black eye?"

Dr. Bradshaw's observation caught Felicia off guard and she didn't know what to say. Felicia thought she had done a pretty good job of covering the bruises on her face with makeup. She didn't think anyone would notice but it was part of Dr. Bradshaw's job to observe people. She was making Felicia uncomfortable the way she was watching her. Felicia was sure Dr. Bradshaw would be able to see right through her, just as Dr. Anderson had but she still lied anyway.

"Yes. I fell down the stairs at home and blacked my eye." Felicia could tell that Dr. Bradshaw didn't believe her.

"I saw you holding your side and wincing when you reached down to pick up my trash can which drew my attention and as I observed you closer that's when I saw your face," she explained.

"Yeah, I bruised my ribs too," Felicia said smiling sheepishly.

"You're name is Felicia right?"

"Yes, my name is Felicia, how'd you know," Felicia asked but she answered her own question as she followed Dr. Bradshaw's gaze towards her work badge.

Instead of replying Dr. Bradshaw asked Felicia the dreaded question that she knew she would surely ask, "Felicia, are you sure that everything is alright with you? Would you like to talk?"

"No," Felicia replied, slightly offended, thinking to herself "Why do people always assume you want to talk about what's bothering you?"

"I'm sorry, I didn't mean to offend you," Dr. Bradshaw tried to apologize.

Felicia softened her tone because she could see that Dr. Bradshaw was genuinely concerned about her.

Felicia smiled and replied, "I'm just clumsy that's all. Please, don't look at me like that," Felicia pleaded with her. "I know what you're thinking and I am telling you that everything is fine."

"Felicia you can trust me. Anything you tell me will be held in the strictest confidence. I have an oath to my patients."

"I don't have anything to talk to you about. Look, I need to get back to work and besides, if I did have anything to say to you I couldn't afford it."

"Well, you look like you could use a little help. How about I help you finish with whatever you have left to cleanup in the building and we can talk while we're working. Free of charge with no strings attached," she replied as she placed her left hand over her heart and raised her left hand as if she were about to recite the pledge of allegiance.

"Why would you do this for me?" Felicia asked skeptically.

"I'm offering to do this for the same reason that you refill the coffee pods in my office; because I want to. I tell you what. I'll start. My name is Melina Bradshaw and I am a clinical psychologist," she said as she offered Felicia a cordial handshake.

"What made you want to become a psychiatrist?" Felicia asked, extending her arm in return to shake Melina's hand.

"I'm a psychologist not a psychiatrist."

Felicia knew she must have sounded really stupid when she asked, "What's the difference?"

"Well the major difference is that a psychiatrist can write prescriptions for medicine while a psychologist cannot. Another difference is that a psychiatrist attends medical school and is a medical doctor while a psychologist attends graduate school and earns a PhD. However, there are a few states that allow psychologists to write prescriptions under the guidance of a psychiatrist but basically those are the differences."

"Oh, I see."

"To answer your previous question, I wanted to be a psychologist because I believe that everyone deserves the right to be happy. I enjoy helping people figure out what's bothering them. I work to help them find solutions to their problems; we work together. I've seen you before Felicia and my instincts are telling me that something is going on with you. I hope you won't be offended but there seems to be a sparkle missing when I look into your eyes. You always seem distant and sad to me. I'm just trying to reach out to you to let you know that I care. I'm here and I would love to help you if I can; if you will allow me to."

Felicia didn't know what to say but in that moment she knew that her life was about to change forever. This was the second time she had been offered help. If her life was ever going to change she was going to need help and she was going to have to trust somebody sometime so why not start with Dr. Bradshaw. It sounded so simple but Felicia needed more time.

Just as she had promised Melina helped Felicia clean the rest of the building while they talked. Actually Melina did most of the talking while Felicia listened. When they were done cleaning the entire building Melina invited Felicia to join her new group that she had just started. She handed Felicia a brochure; the same one Felicia had thrown away a couple of weeks ago. Felicia new this had to be a sign that maybe she needed to hold on to the brochure this time so she tucked it away in her cleaning cart.

"Felicia, I hope you will be able to attend the women's group I have starting next Thursday. It's free and if you want to come next week and just listen that will be fine. No strings attached. We'll meet every other Thursday."

"I can't make any promises but I will seriously consider your offer." This time Felicia was telling the truth. She was going to give Melina's offer to join the women's group serious consideration.

"Fair enough," Melina said smiling.

"Thank you for helping me get my work done and I really enjoyed spending time talking with you."

"Felicia, the pleasure was mine."

"Have a good evening Dr. Bradshaw."

"I will and you have a good evening as well."

They said good night one last time when the elevator stopped on the third floor. Felicia caught a glimpse of her reflection in the elevator doors when they closed shut and she couldn't suppress the overwhelming urge to smile. She was terrified but for the first time in a very long time she felt hopeful.

Felicia looked at her watch and realized that with Dr. Bradshaw's help she had finished her work a whole hour early. But she couldn't go home just yet because she wouldn't be able to explain why she had gotten off work so early. She thought about going to get a cup of coffee but she dismissed that idea because Marcus would see the extra mileage on the car in the morning and that wouldn't be good either. So instead, she spent the extra hour sitting in her car reflecting on the events that had just transpired that evening; pondering whether or not Dr. Bradshaw would really be able to help her.

CHAPTER 7

Naomi

A Date With Destiny

Naomi called Lance a couple of days later. She didn't want to appear too eager, however, she didn't want to leave him with the impression that she was not interested at all because she was definitely interested. Preparing to leave a message on his voicemail after the fourth ring, she was surprised when he actually answered the phone.

"May I speak with Mr. Lance Davenport?"

"Hello Naomi. You don't have to be so formal. You can call me Lance."

For a brief second Naomi was taken aback when Lance greeted her by name. She was a little bewildered as to how he knew it was her calling him. Then it dawned on her that her name must have appeared in the caller id.

"So this is your legitimate number?" she teased.

"I beg your pardon?" Lance asked, feigning to be offended. "I wouldn't have given you my number if I didn't want you to call me."

"I'm sorry. I didn't mean it like that. It's just that I never would have assumed this was your personal phone number. I was expecting to speak with your assistant or answering service. You just caught me off guard when you answered the phone, that's all," Naomi explained.

"I consider our conversation to be of a personal nature and I handle all of my personal affairs directly," he said.

"Oh, I see," she replied. She was impressed. "Well, obviously, I looked on the back of your business card and found your phone number, otherwise I wouldn't be calling. However, I was a little curious about the other information that was on the back of the card. Were you inviting me somewhere," Naomi inquired?

"Yes, I was inviting you out on a date."

"A date, huh? Well why didn't you just come out and ask me for a date when you were in the office the other day?"

"I didn't want to put either one of us on the spot so I figured if you were the least bit interested, or curious, you would call. If you didn't call then there would be no harm, no foul committed by either party."

"Well, Mr. Davenport, I mean, Lance, let me say that I am very interested in going out on a date with you."

"Excellent. Give me your address and I will have my chauffer pick you up on Saturday evening."

"Lance, please don't take this the wrong way. I really appreciate the offer of your chauffer picking me up, but how about I just meet you there."

"I understand," Lance chuckled. "I will meet you at my restaurant on Saturday. Just give the Maitre d' your name and tell him that you are my special guest. Until then I'll look forward to seeing you there"

"I look forward to our date too and I'll see you on Saturday," Naomi said, very nonchalantly in an effort to contain her excitement.

To say that Naomi was excited would be an understatement. She was ecstatic to be going out on a date with Mr. Lance Davenport. She just didn't know how she was going to manage the long wait until Saturday. She definitely had to find something else to occupy her time until then so she scheduled an appointment to get her hair done, a manicure & pedicure, and her eyebrows waxed. These appointments wouldn't be enough to keep her from thinking about Lance but at least it was better than doing nothing at all.

In Naomi's opinion every woman should have two main staples in her wardrobe; a little black dress and a sexy red dress. A date with a man like Lance required her sexy red dress because it fit her body like a glove, it commanded attention, and it was made to seduce a man. She wanted Lance Davenport and she meant to have him; tonight.

Even though Naomi was already five feet ten inches tall she still liked to wear a nice high heeled shoe. It generally wasn't a problem because she preferred men over six feet tall. In Lance's case a four inch heeled shoe would put her almost at eye level with him. Yet another advantage she had learned from Mr. Larosa.

Thanks to her height, exercise and healthy eating she had a very lean body with curves in all the right places. She had been blessed with flawless, caramel colored skin from her mother. Her complexion was a result of the mixture of her African American, Native American, and European heritage.

Naomi decided to wear her hair in a long cascade of curls swept to one side, neatly secured with bobby pins at the nape of her neck. She applied eye shadow and mascara for a smoky effect and finished the look with red lipstick to match her dress. All she had left to do was grab her red peep toe pumps from the closet and she was ready to go.

Davenport's was an upscale restaurant rightly named after its owner. Lance had built his restaurant in downtown Raleigh as part of the city's revitalization project. The entrance leading up to the restaurant was adorned on both sides with miniature coach lamps to light the pathway.

The front doors were flanked on either side by two men who looked like they were some type of mythical Greek Adonis. They opened the doors welcoming Naomi inside the restaurant and immediately she felt as if she had been transformed to another place. She couldn't believe she had never dined at Davenports before but once she stepped inside she was glad she hadn't. There was something extraordinary about being here for the first time to meet Lance.

Behind the Maitre d' stand was a waterfall that gave the illusion of water falling from the ceiling and mysteriously disappearing into the floor below. The sound of the water flowing, in concert with the light illuminating through it, was very tranquil which provided a very calming effect upon entering the restaurant.

The Maitre d' extended his arm and escorted her to a private dining room when he discovered that she was Lance's special guest. He made Naomi feel as if she were royalty.

The view took her breath away when he opened the door and she stepped inside the private dining area. In the center of the room, directly beneath an enormous crystal chandelier stood a round table with place settings set for a king. It was the only table in the entire room. They had their own private waiter who appeared to stand on guard to fulfill their every whim. It projected a scene straight out of the pages of some enchanted fairy tale.

Lance pulled out all the stops for their first date. They started the evening off with a bottle of champagne while feasting on caviar, bacon wrapped scallops, and crab stuffed mushrooms for appetizers. For their main course they dined on filet mignon smothered in an asiago and cracked peppercorn cream sauce, lobster tails, asparagus tips, and sweet potato soufflé, followed by white chocolate bread pudding drizzled with caramel sauce for dessert.

Lance folded his napkin when they were done eating and walked around to Naomi's side of the table. He extended his hand towards her and she placed her hand in his. As if on cue, the jazz music that they had listened to while dining transitioned over to smooth R & B. Lance guided her towards the dance floor and embraced her in a dance. She rested her head on his shoulder while they danced to the romantic music that was playing softly throughout the room. She closed her eyes as he held her and they let their bodies sway to the rhythm of the music. Naomi felt as though she had died and gone to heaven. The only thing that could make this date any better would be waking up in the morning with Lance lying next to her in her bed.

With that thought she knew it was time for her to put her plan into action and make her move to seduce Lance. Reaching up to place both of her hands behind his back she pulled her body in closer towards his. Everything about Lance exuded style and class; even his cologne smelled expensive. She took a few moments just to bask in his aroma and to relish in the warmth of his embrace.

Their personal waiter had left the room soon after he finished serving them their dessert, leaving Lance and Naomi alone in the room. Moving forward with her plans she reached up and kissed Lance on the lips. Sensing no resistance she opened her mouth deepening their kiss. He relentlessly returned her kisses as passionately as she was kissing him. So she was thoroughly disappointed when Lance was the first one to break their embrace and escorted her back to the table.

"So have you enjoyed yourself this evening?" Lance inquired.

"Yes I have. Thank you Lance, this night has been better than I could ever imagine."

"Good. I am glad that you have enjoyed yourself because I have enjoyed the pleasure of your company as well." When Lance did not pull out her chair for her to sit back down Naomi suddenly realized that their date was coming to an end. "So, are you ready to go?" he asked.

Hell no, she wasn't ready to go, but what else could she say? "Sure", she found herself saying, staring at him in utter disbelief that he was ending their date so soon. She had been thoroughly enjoying the evening with Lance and she was positive he was as well. So she put a smile on her face and pretended not to be perturbed.

"Why don't I ride home with you to make sure you get home safely and I'll have my chauffer follow us?"

"Thank you! That sounds like a great idea," Naomi replied. "So he isn't ending our date. I see, he has plans to go back to my place afterall," she thought to herself. Lance smiled down at her as they walked arm and arm through the restaurant and out the front door. Naomi was glowing on the inside but she didn't want to show it so she bit her bottom lip to keep her smile from radiating all over her face. The valet pulled her car around and she suggested Lance drive. She wanted a chance to examine him more. What better opportunity could she have to observe him than to have Lance drive her home?

When they reached the front door of her condo she turned towards Lance to speak to him before putting her key in the lock.

"I'm so glad you decided to see that I made it home safely. Why don't you go ahead and dismiss your chauffer and I'll drive you home in the morning," she suggested. His next words left her flabbergasted. She felt like she had been doused with a bucket of cold water.

"As inviting as your offer may sound, I am afraid I have to decline. I really enjoyed our date this evening Naomi," he said as he reached down, kissed her on the cheek and said goodnight.

Sensing her disappointment he tried to explain, "I wish our date didn't have to end so soon but I have to get up very early in the morning. I hope you understand"

"No I don't understand!" Naomi wanted to scream at the top of her lungs but instead she replied, "Sure I understand".

How could he be walking away from her and all she had to offer? She was practically throwing herself at him and yet he refused to take the bait. Most women Naomi knew had a three month rule. Well she had a one date rule. If a man passed the test during the first date they were going to finish the evening either at his place, her place or a hotel. This was the first time she had ever been turned down when she was clearly the one who had made the first move and she didn't like it.

She watched in disbelief as Lance stepped into his limo and just like that he was gone. She had to admit to herself that her ego was slightly wounded. She didn't expect very much from men so she was perplexed, to say the least, that he had turned down her obvious advances.

She wanted Lance now, more than ever. "Was this some ploy of his? Was he trying to use reverse psychology on me?" Naomi thought to herself. Well, he didn't know who he was dealing with. Little did he know that Naomi knew how to use what her mama gave her and she was determined now more than ever to beat him at his own game.

CHAPTER 8

Melina

You Can Lead A Horse To Water

Perception *[per-sep-shuh n] - Cognitive understand-*

ing; insight; intuition; or discernment.

Melina was relieved when the session with her last patient of the day was finally over. Not because she didn't enjoy her job and didn't want to hear what her patients had to say. In fact she took her job very seriously but today her thoughts were preoccupied with the group session she was going to have later that evening with the women who had suddenly become "unofficial" patients of hers.

She kept thinking about Felicia; wondering if she would even show up. Melina knew that Felicia had to work tonight which meant that technically she would be in the building but that didn't mean that she would join the group. In her heart of hearts Melina knew that Felicia was struggling with abuse. Melina wanted so desperately to be able to help her but one thing she had learned over the years is that you can only help people who want to be helped. Until they are willing to admit to an issue or commit to resolving it you are really just wasting your time.

But the physical evidence didn't lie no matter what Felicia said. No one got bruises like that on their face from falling down a flight of stairs and especially not the black eye she had. That kind of bruising could only come from being hit with a fist. Melina had observed too many cases of domestic violence not to know the signs. Although Felicia did a pretty good job of covering it up, this was not the first time Melina had observed bruises on Felicia. There had been a couple of other times before this most recent incident so Melina was certain that this wouldn't be the last.

In Melina's opinion, Felicia always appeared very demure to her. She was friendly enough but she always had a look of sadness in her eyes. Melina discerned a lot of pain from Felicia which may have attributed to her somewhat reclusive personality. Melina just prayed that Felicia would come to the meeting.

There was about an hour and a half before the session was supposed to begin. Melina's receptionist had already left for the evening so she opened her office door so that she would be able to see the ladies when they arrived. Once Melina felt everything was in place and ready to her satisfaction she sat down on the new sofa and excitedly, yet nervously waited for each one of them to arrive.

She was a tad bit anxious because she wasn't sure how many of the women would even show up. She knew that her niece Tanisha would be there. Her niece was a junior in college at North Carolina Central University, in Durham, NC and Melina had given her an internship working in her office. This support group would be Tanisha's practicum.

Melina was roused out of her musing when she heard the outer door leading to the reception area open at five thirty. It was her niece Tanisha. Melina was very pleased to see that her niece had arrived early but she hadn't really expected anything different. Being early demonstrated her niece's professionalism. It showed Melina that Tanisha was taking her internship very seriously and wasn't being presumptuous or taking advantage of the situation and the fact that they were family.

After they finished talking, Tanisha helped her Aunt Melina light a few candles throughout the office to create a tranquil aura. Melina also decided to burn a few oils as well to provide a pleasant aroma. Kandi arrived with another woman whom Melina assumed was her friend Naomi that she had mentioned she was going to bring. They introduced themselves before Melina invited the women to take a seat and offered them something to drink while they waited for the other two women to join them.

As they were waiting for Susan and Felicia to arrive, Melina noticed that Naomi kept checking her watch, tapping her foot, and running her hand across her forehead to move a piece of hair out of her face that wasn't really there. These were all signs of nervousness, impatience, or being somewhere you didn't want to be. Melina wasn't sure which one it was; perhaps a little bit of each. Naomi didn't strike her as the nervous type. In fact she carried herself with a confidence that bordered on the brink of arrogance. However, as a therapist it was Melina's job to keep an open mind and not be too quick to categorize people without getting to know them first. Besides, Melina doubted very seriously that anyone could make Naomi do anything that she didn't really want to do so Melina decided to give her the benefit of the doubt.

Susan arrived at six fifty-five and everyone was there except for Felicia. Melina would give her five more minutes and then start promptly at seven o'clock. She valued the women's time and did not want to waste it. Two things Melina believed in were being on time and starting on time. She had to be punctual in her practice as well. Otherwise, her entire schedule could be thrown out of kilter. Unfortunately for that very reason, if a patient were late Melina had no choice but to keep on schedule by ending each session on time. She could not extend their session into another patient's allotted time because she always had another patient waiting. Most of her patients realized this and wanted to utilize their entire session so they were generally always on time.

They were just about to get started when Felicia came walking through the door. Melina had almost given up hope that Felicia was going to make it so she was very happy to see her. Felicia had actually shown up and now everyone was there.

CHAPTER 9

Tanisha

Divine Intervention

Even though they lived less than an hour apart it seemed that once Tanisha started college she rarely got a chance to see her Aunt Melina as often as she used to. She was so overjoyed that her aunt was allowing her to work in her office on an internship. Although Tanisha would not be working with Melina specifically on any of her client cases the experience she was going to gain working with Melina's pro bono group was still invaluable training. An added plus was that the sessions were in the evening which fit Tanisha's school schedule and meeting every other week allowed her to take a full class load this semester.

Tanisha had her own car so there wasn't an issue with making the forty-five minute commute between Durham, NC and Raleigh, NC. Melina wanted this to be a rewarding experience for her niece so she compensated Tanisha for her gas on top of the salary she was going to pay her. Tanisha realized how blessed she was to have this opportunity because most internships within her field were unpaid. Her aunt always spoiled her for as long as she could remember. For Tanisha this was a win-win situation that she was very grateful for.

Tanisha had made it a point to arrive early for the first session so that she would have a few minutes to catch up and talk with her aunt alone. She also wanted to allow a little extra time in case her aunt needed to review anything with her in private before the other women arrived. Tanisha had always loved the architecture of the building where her aunt's office was located. It had so many architectural angles and eighty-five percent of the building was made of glass. The lobby of the building had always made Tanisha feel as if she were stepping into an art museum. In fact, several of the paintings on the walls were actual donations as well as several sculptures and pottery pieces.

There was plenty of natural light shining through the glass along with recessed and track lighting that illuminated and enhanced all of the art pieces. Reminiscing now, Tanisha remembered the day she had looked in every nook and cranny of the lobby one Saturday afternoon when her aunt first moved into this building. She had been in the process of decorating her office that day and Tanisha had come along to keep her company. Being careful not to touch anything, as tempting as it had been, Tanisha had meticulously perused each and every piece of artwork, sculpture and pottery in the entire lobby.

Some of the pieces of art were by local NC artists. Tanisha particularly remembered one piece of art that drew her attention that day. It was a piece by African American muralist John Thomas Biggers. Tanisha didn't really know anything about art but his artwork intrigued her for some reason that she couldn't explain. A couple of years later her parents took her to an exhibition of his art collection featured at Gaston College in his birthplace of Gastonia, NC and she was able to meet Mr. Biggers in person.

Tanisha got off the elevator on her aunt's floor and smiled at the memory. It was ironic that she hadn't been to Melina's office in years but she still remembered it like it was yesterday. She knew that her aunt had recently redecorated her office. Tanisha thought that her aunt always had such good decorating tastes so she was extremely excited to see all the changes her aunt had made in her office.

"Hi Auntie", Tanisha said, walking towards her aunt with opens arms to embrace her in a hug.

"Hey Niecey", Melina replied, returning Tanisha's embrace and kissing her on the cheek. "How have you been?"

"I've been great Auntie. I missed you!"

"I missed you too! So when did you decide to cut off all your hair?"

"Oh, about a month ago. Why? You don't like it?" Tanisha asked while spinning around in order for her Aunt to get a full view of her new hairstyle.

"Actually I do. I hate to see all your lovely hair gone but this style is very becoming on you."

"I decided to embrace my "natural" hair."

"Well I'm glad you did, welcome to the natural side", Melina said patting her hair as if she had just finished styling it.

They both laughed. Melina had been trying to convince Tanisha to go natural for years now. Tanisha vowed she would never let go of the "creamy crack" but several of her friends had gone natural so she decided to give a try. Tanisha figured at the very least if she didn't like her hair she could let it grow out and perm it again but to her surprise she really loved her hair in its natural state.

"I hope you don't mind but I decided to come a little early so that we could have a little time to talk and I wasn't sure if there was anything you might want to go over with me before the session starts", Tanisha explained to her aunt.

"Girl, stop being silly, you know good and well that I don't mind you coming early. As a matter of fact, I'm glad you did", Melina replied. "You know I am dying to hear all about your summer trip to Spain! So come on over here and have a seat so you can tell me all about it," Melina said, patting the empty space on the sofa next to her.

"Ok, I will Auntie but first I want to have a look around your new office. Wow, Auntie! It's so beautiful. I feel like I am on some exotic tropical island, spa retreat but yet I feel warm and cozy at the same time like I'm on a mountain cabin retreat."

"Great, because that was the look and feel I was going for," Melina remarked.

They both laughed. Tanisha finished looking around the office before she grabbed her photo album that chronicled her trip to Spain and took a seat on the new couch. She enjoyed reliving the experiences from the photos as she filled her aunt in on all the details of her summer trip to Spain. It felt so good to Tanisha to be able to talk to her aunt again in person.

They were engrossed in conversation when the door to Melina's outer office was opened. She got up to greet Kandi and Naomi who had arrived while Tanisha put the photo album back into her backpack and pulled out her notepad and pen. Melina made small talk with the women as they arrived to the office. She officially started the meeting at seven o'clock on the dot after Felicia arrived.

"I would like to introduce everyone to my niece Tanisha", Melina said, introducing Tanisha to the women's group. "She is a college student at North Carolina Central University majoring in psychology. She will be joining us to use these sessions as her clinical practicum for internship experience".

"Hi", Tanisha replied. "Thank you for allowing me to be a part of this group and to observe your sessions. You can rest assured that anything discussed in these meetings will be held in the strictest confidence. Even though I am a student I am bound by a confidentiality agreement as part of the terms of my internship and involvement with this group. I am looking forward to working with you and getting to know each of you better. I am positive that this will be a memorable experience and I will be gaining invaluable training from this internship."

"Dr. Bradshaw is my dad's baby sister. Well, actually she is his only sister. She is my role model and she is the reason that I went to college to study psychology. I admire her and the work she does. I commend her desire to reach out and help others and I want to follow in her footsteps."

Melina was beaming as Tanisha boasted about her while explaining the dynamics of their relationship to the other women. It was clear to see the and they had no objections to her being a part of the group. As Tanisha looked around the circle she sensed that they were all a little apprehensive and she respected how brave they were because it took a lot of courage for them to be there. She smiled at Melina and made a mental note to thank her aunt again for inviting her to participate in this group.

Tanisha observed Felicia who was seated next to Melina picking at her fingernails and barely making eye contact with anyone since she had arrived. Felicia's nervousness was more apparent than anyone else in the room. Melina patted Felicia on the hand and reassured her that everything would be ok. The tension eased from Felicia's body as she relaxed in her seat and began introducing herself to the group. Felicia told them her name. She paused for a moment, took a deep breath, closed her eyes, and then all of a sudden, as if someone had magically turned on a switch inside of her body, her demeanor changed. Her entire disposition transformed as she began telling them about her children. Her face radiated when she spoke about them and it was obvious to anyone just how much she loved her kids.

One by one each woman introduced herself. It would eventually take some time for them to open up fully about their lives but tonight was a start. This was an exceptional group of women and Tanisha knew that God had placed all of them here at this appointed place, at this appointed time, including her. She had an overwhelming sense that this was definitely going to be an experience she would never forget for the rest of her life.

CHAPTER 10

Felicia

Confessions and Release

Awareness *[uh-wair-nis] - The state or condition of be-*

ing aware; having knowledge; consciousness.

Even though it had been three months since the initial meet-ing, Felicia still couldn't believe that she had actually accepted Melina's invitation to join the support group. Up until now she had been grateful that she had joined but tonight she wasn't so sure. During the meetings so far, Melina had done most of the talking and the women had basically done small talk and exercises to get to know one another better. Felicia had been fine with that.

However, at the end of the last session Melina had informed them that during the next meeting they were going to delve deeper.

Felicia wasn't very good at expressing her intimate feelings which was making her very nervous but she was here so she couldn't very well leave now.

She just hoped that she would actually be able to open herself up in front of these women and discuss things that she had never even been able to discuss with her own family. She had been isolated from other people for so long that keeping things bottled up inside of her seemed normal. She didn't think it was possible to share her ordeal with anyone else without feeling totally embarrassed and humiliated. So instead she had learned to just live with her shame.

Felicia inherently became aware of the silence in the room and realized they were all staring at her, waiting for her to start. She knew that she had to say something. They weren't complete strangers anymore but there was still a lot that they didn't know about each other. Where did she even begin?

Hesitantly, Felicia turned to look over at Melina who was seated next to her on her right. Melina patted Felicia on the hand reassuringly before speaking, "Its ok Felicia. Just take a deep. Take your time and start from the beginning whenever you are ready."

"Well, of course y'all already know that I'm married and I have three kids, so I guess I don't need to start there," Felicia began. Felicia's heart always radiated with happiness whenever she talked about her children because they were her pride and joy. The best part of her life was her children. They were her only reason for living.

Did she dare tell these women the intimate details of how her life had fallen apart? How her entire life with Marcus had been a living nightmare. She suddenly felt herself overwhelmed again with fear at the thought of sharing her pain with these women who were only acquaintances at best. But she knew she had to say something. They were expecting her to say something. Isn't that why she had come here in the first place?

An inner voice deep down inside of Felicia was crying out for help and as fearful as she was she could not pass up this opportunity that had been granted to her. She had to start somewhere so it might as well be here and she might as well start from the beginning as Melina had suggested. Felicia diverted their glances by staring down at her feet which somehow made it more comfortable for her to begin. Taking a deep breath she reluctantly began to tell her story…

Instead of going to the prom, going on my senior class trip or going to college, I graduated from high school, got married at the county court house, and gave birth to my first child two months later; all in that order," Felicia stated rather matter-of-factly, as if she were reading off a list of task on a to do list. She couldn't help it because that's what her life felt like; a miserable existence of mundane tasks and routines.

She raised her eyes to meet the gazes of the other women in the room and to her relief they were not looking at her condescendingly. Instead, she saw sympathy and compassion which alleviated her apprehension and made her feel at ease. She didn't know it just yet but the veil of dark ugly secrets that she had been hiding behind all these years was finally about to be removed.

"Marcus and I first met in high school. He was a star athlete on the football team. I have to admit that I was a little surprised when he wanted to date me. I mean don't get me wrong, I had my fair share of friends but I wasn't a cheerleader, overly popular or anything like that. I didn't know that he was even aware I existed because we didn't travel in the same circle. He said he had been watching me for a while and he actually admired the fact that I wasn't trying to get with him like all the other girls in our school were.

In the beginning of our relationship I was a little skeptical why he had chosen me, but he always made me feel like I was the one. He was sweet, and kind, and charming. He made me feel special and I quickly found myself infatuated with him. I was falling deeply in love with him and I felt that he was falling in love with me too. Everyone knew he was at the top of his game in football and he was going places. Suddenly, I found myself surrounded with so many new friends. People that had barely even spoken to me before in the past were trying to be friends with me now. I knew that most of them were only being nice to me because of my association with Marcus but I have to admit that I met some really genuine people too.

We became inseparable and even though we were only in high school I knew that this was more than puppy love. We were on top of the world. The feelings I felt for Marcus were real and genuine. For the first time in my life I knew what it felt like to be loved by a man. What I didn't realize at the time was that Marcus was not a man. In fact he was still a boy and my idea of love was very different from his.

I didn't see the other side of Marcus until our senior year in high school. It was the state championship football game. Marcus had everything riding on this game. He lived, ate, and breathed football. Marcus took a hit late in the third quarter. When the play was over he didn't get up. In fact he wasn't moving.

There was complete silence throughout the entire stadium as if everyone was holding their breath. It was so quiet that you could literally hear a pin drop. All eyes were glued to the field. Generally the band would play something in an event like this to keep the fans preoccupied but even they weren't playing. I felt as if my heart had stopped beating as I watched the events unfolding before my eyes.

The paramedics were summoned to assist the team trainer. The game was delayed for what felt like an eternity. Marcus was finally secured on a stretcher and he gave the thumbs up signaling that everything was going to be ok; but everything wasn't ok. Just like that, Marcus's career was over. One play, one hit and his future in football was over. Marcus had suffered neck and back injuries.

Initially it was feared that his injuries might leave him paralyzed from the neck down. Miraculously, within a couple of weeks, Marcus regained complete control of his limbs and made a full recovery but his career was still over. He was informed that if he continued to play football he would be playing Russian roulette with his life. To make matters worse, his college football scholarship was rescinded and I had just found out that I was pregnant with our son DeMarcus.

Football was Marcus's life and without it his whole personality changed. He was in a terrible mood all the time and I quickly became the target of his anger. On the day that I told him I was pregnant with his child he tried to talk me into having an abortion. When I refused to get rid of our baby he back handed me across the face so hard that he busted my lip. That's the day the abuse began and that's the day that I started hiding it from the rest of the world.

As soon as I got home I put ice on my lip to keep it from swelling any further. In fact, I held the ice on my lip for so long until my lip became numb and it felt as if I had been given a double dose of Novocaine. I had to get the swelling down because my mother would have hit the roof if she had found out that Marcus had hit me.

My mother did not take mess from anybody and especially not from a man. She also did not believe in second chances. There was no three strike rule with my mother. You got one chance and one chance only. You've heard the motto: "Fool me once shame on you, fool me twice shame on me"? Well my mother's version was: "Fool me once shame on me because you will never get another chance to fool me again".

My mother wore the apron and the pants in our house and she wasn't afraid to let anyone know it; especially my dad. She treated my dad like he was one of the kids. My father may have been a little weak when it came to standing up to her, but in his defense, no man really stood a chance with my mother because in her eyes she didn't need a man. Losing his job was the straw that broke the camel's back for both of them.

Being out of work and unable to provide for his family broke his spirit and my daddy was never the same after that. It's like a part of him died along with his dream and my mother never let him forget it. He eventually turned to drinking. A lot of people become boisterous and belligerent when they drink but my father became the total opposite. He became solemn and withdrawn. It was as if he had mentally checked out on life. When he could no longer hold down a job she kicked him out of the house and he never came back.

My dad ended up moving to Washington, DC to live with his brother. He would only work off and on in order to make enough money to support his drinking habit. My uncle's wife eventually got fed up and said he had to go because she couldn't have him getting drunk all night and then laying around her house all day so he inevitably moved into a rooming house.

My daddy ended up getting mugged in an alley one night when he was walking home from a bar. No one found his body until the next day and by then it was too late. He was already dead.

I guess that's why I have taken Marcus's abuse for so long. I didn't want my children to grow up without having a real family and knowing their father. So, I tried to go out of my way to be nurturing and supportive of my husband. I let him be the king of his castle. Refusing to drive my husband away the way my mother had done my father, I was subservient and he took advantage of me. Eventually Marcus became so mean and violent that my submissiveness evolved into fear of him and before I knew it this just became a way of life. Now, I live in fear of my husband and I try everything in my power not to evoke his wrath"…

When Felicia looked up this time she could see pity, shock and disbelief in their eyes. Everyone was crying except for Naomi. As she looked around the room at each one of these women, Felicia could see the concern they had for her. She could feel the love flowing from each tear they were crying and she felt stronger. Even though Naomi wasn't crying Felicia could still see compassion in her eyes. They shared something. Felicia felt that Naomi understood the harshness of her life better than any of the other women in the room, with perhaps the exception of Melina.

Felicia's deep dark secret was finally out. Her mother and family didn't even know about the abuse she had suffered through all these year. She had just crossed the first hurdle and she knew that her life would never be the same. Somehow she drew strength from these women that she never knew she had within her. A heavy weight had been lifted from her shoulders and she was so thankful.

CHAPTER 11

Naomi

I'm A Survivor

Of course Naomi felt sorry for Felicia when she heard her story but she had pain of her own to deal with. Her story was just as sad and tragic as Felicia's was. It wasn't a coincidence that Kandi had finally convinced her to join this group. Naomi had known for a long time now that the only way she was going to be able to move forward with her life was to come to terms with her past. As painful and as unpleasant as it was she too had to go back to the beginning. She had to reopen some wounds that she had tried to bury a long time ago because they were still there. She didn't actually realize how deeply she had buried some of those hurts until after she had finished talking…

"I had heard the same thing over and over again my entire life like a broken record. Everyone always told me that I was looking for love in all the wrong places. Even though it was so cliché I knew it was so true. As human beings, all we want and need is to feel loved. It's in our nature. But somehow I never found love in any of the usual places it should have been found. So instead I sought love wherever I could find it. I had been trying to find real love for so long until one day I eventually came to the realization that love wasn't in the cards for me and at that point I stopped caring. My philosophy on life became "I'm gonna get mine before you get yours". I basically stopped worrying about other people and started pursuing the things that made ME happy, no matter the cost.

I guess my trouble with love began the day I was born, or better yet conceived. My mother was a beautiful woman who could get any man she wanted. The problem was the man she wanted didn't want her and I paid the price for it. She never really wanted me. I was just a pawn in her game. In the end I turned out to be more of an inconvenience when her plan to trap my father into marriage backfired in her face. To my mother I was a constant reminder of the man who didn't want her, so in return, she didn't want me.

That was cool though. I quickly learned to find other ways to get the love that my mother couldn't or wouldn't give me. I quickly learned to use my assets to get what I wanted out of life. I refused to be a victim in this game called love. Let's just say that I used what my mama gave me to my advantage; good looks and natural born sex appeal. The only difference between me and my mother was I was never stupid enough to fall in love.

I left home when I was 16 and I've never looked back. I felt like I had been all alone my entire life so I had nothing to keep me there. In fact, I had every reason to leave. My mother had so much contempt for me and treated me like her own personal slave until I felt like I was a prisoner in my own home. The only people who showed me any affection were the boys at school. Of course I knew deep down inside that it wasn't really affection but when you're searching for something, you see what you want to see whether it's real or not.

The girls at school all hated me because I was pretty. They always regarded me as a threat. My mother wouldn't let me have any friends and I was an only child so I had no one to talk to. Most people in my situation would have gone crazy out of their mind but I had a strong will to survive. So, I suffered alone in my misery biding my time until that day I packed everything I owned in my suitcase and left town.

When I first got the notion to leave home, I had no idea where I was going to go. I just knew that when the time came I was getting as far away from my mother as I could. I had thought about going to the west coast but something about California scared me. I kept thinking about those men stalking the bus stations and airports looking for gullible unsuspecting young girls that they could string out on drugs and force into a life of prostitution. Now of course I was not some little naïve country girl coming from Podunk Mississippi so I knew that wasn't going to happen to me. I knew how to survive and take care of myself so I settled on going to New York.

Now don't get me wrong, New York can be a scary place too, but somehow I found comfort in the knowledge that New York was closer to home than California which gave me a sense of security. Not that I had any intentions of ever going back home but the East Coast offered familiarity.

Before I left home I had already found a studio apartment in a three bedroom brownstone in Brooklyn, NY for five hundred and fifty dollars a month with utilities included. I knew that going to a big city could be expensive but I had started working when I was fourteen. I had saved every dime I ever earned waiting for this day. My decision to leave home was not some random, haphazard decision. Even though I didn't know exactly where I was going I had made up my mind to leave a long time ago and I simply waited until I had saved up enough money to last me for about a year on my own.

My plans were to find a job and go to school at night to finish my GED. I knew that leaving home before I graduated high school was risky but it was a risk I was willing to take. I didn't have time to wait two more years. If I was going to do this it was going to be now or never. I could get my GED and after a year of living on my own I would be able to qualify for grants to go to college in the city. I needed to be in a city where it would be easy to get around on public transportation. So, New York seemed to be the ideal place for me to go. The apartment I found was only three blocks away from the Clinton/Washington G train and half a block away from the B54 and B61 bus lines near Dekalb and Washington Avenues. I had it all figured out.

Once I arrived in New York and saw the apartment I immediately understood why the rent was only five hundred and fifty dollars. To list this space as a studio apartment was an understatement or better yet an overstatement. It was more like a closet with a window. As a matter of fact I am sure that there are some people who have closets bigger than that quote, un-quote apartment. There was only enough room for a single bed, night stand, dresser and dormitory sized refrigerator. There was barely enough room for me to pull out the drawers of the dresser without bumping into the mattress. I could literally sit on the side of the bed and pull out the drawers just enough to reach my legs. The same was true when opening the door of the refrigerator. There were two shared kitchens and two shared bathrooms for all of the tenants of the brownstone. It was tiny to say the least, but it was better than living on the street and it was mine.

I spent the first few days learning my way around the city. The following week I landed a job as a waitress at a diner around the corner from the brownstone that served breakfast, lunch and brunch. My plan was to use the money I made working at the diner to pay for my day to day living expenses and use the money I had saved up to pay my rent. I enrolled in an evening GED course for the fall at Medgar Evers College off Bedford Avenue which would later become the learning institution where I earned my associates degree in Public Administration. All my plans were coming to fruition and for the first time in my life I felt as if I was living on top of the world but you know what they say about New York…

"New York can be a big city of dreams, but be careful, because sometimes everything in New York is not what it seems".

CHAPTER 12

Susan

"Him"

When it was Susan's turn to speak she was more than eager. She wasn't leery about sharing her feelings with them; she felt just the opposite. Susan figured "why not". She was feeling angry and confused about the whole situation with Larry and his son. She had a million questions racing through her mind and she felt like she was going crazy worrying about it. She needed desperately to talk to someone and she couldn't talk to her best friend right now; her husband. She needed someone to listen to her and to help her figure out what was going on. To be honest she was looking for an ally to validate all of the doubts about her husband that were consuming her every waking hour. She needed someone to be her voice of reason so she decided to turn to these women.

These women didn't know Susan and oddly enough that gave her courage because she didn't care what they thought of her. She just wanted their honest opinions and because they didn't really know her she felt that they wouldn't sugar coat their answers. They would give it to her straight and keep it real as they say.

Of course she trusted her husband, yet, at the same time there was something deep, down inside, telling Susan that Larry wasn't being completely truthful with her. It was just a feeling that she couldn't shake. Call it women's intuition, but something in her spirit just didn't feel right and she knew if she was ever going to have any peace she had to get to the bottom of it.

Susan had no respect for a man who could walk away from his children. Her own father had walked away from his family when she was a child and so had Larry's dad. That's why she and Larry had both been so devoted to their children. She loved her husband but in her book love and respect went hand in hand. Likewise, love and trust go hand in hand. With no trust there is no love and she just couldn't love someone if she didn't have respect for them. Susan was fully aware that a marriage without respect can deteriorate over time and she did not want that to happen to her marriage. So as far as she was concerned she didn't have anything to lose.

Melina was right. If they were going to share intimate details of their lives they had to be relaxed with one another. Susan removed the pillow that was supporting her back and placed it in her lap so that she could be more comfortable and began to share with them the real reason why she had become a part of this group…

"My husband and I just found out fairly recently that he may have a son. Susan noticed a couple of the women's eyes widen. It happened before we were together but I am still having a hard time with this news. He says that he didn't know that he had a child but I'm not so sure that I believe him. I don't know what I will do if

I find out that he knew about his son and walked away from him. I guess timing is everything because when I met Melina for lunch a few months ago she told me about this group and asked me if I wanted to come. I said yes because I needed someone to talk to.

I know this all probably sounds crazy but I just can't help it. I'm finding myself losing trust and respect for my husband. This has been eating away at me and that's why I am here. I can't help but feel sorry for my husband's son because I know what kind of a life my children had growing up with their father. What I really can't understand is: how Larry could do this. I just can't respect any man who would knowingly walk out on his kids. My father did that to me and my brother. Then he had the unmitigated gall to walk back into our lives twenty nine years later as if nothing ever happened.

I met my father for the first time that I could remember when I was thirty-one years old because he left when I was a toddler. I grew up during a time when it wasn't uncommon for a man to say, "Baby, I'm going to the store for milk, cigarettes and a loaf of bread", and never come back. It was also an era where personal records and information were not readily attainable with a few keystrokes of a computer so it was very easy for people to just disappear and never be found if they didn't want to be. All of that has changed now and I know it is much easier to find people through records and research.

Actually my mother was the one who found my father after he had been missing for nearly twenty-nine years. She wanted to find her long lost love. She wanted to rekindle the romance they once shared. She had mentioned it to me and my brother but I never thought she would really go through with it, much less actually find him. My mouth almost literally dropped to the floor when she sat me and my brother down to share the news that she had found him and he had agreed to meet us. The moment was so surreal. Over the years I had imagined what he might look like and what type of person he might be. Now I actually had the opportunity to meet him.

In the beginning I was excited and embraced the idea of re-uniting with my father again. Where had he been all these years? Did he still love us? Had he been trying to find us; Did he have other children? Another family perhaps? I couldn't wait to meet him and introduce him to my family. How would he feel about meeting his grandkids for the first time?

I was finally going to meet this other person who had made me. I was the spitting image of my mother and everyone always said my brother resembled our father so I only had a small inkling of what he might look like. Unfortunately my mother had not saved a single photo of my father after he walked out of our lives so I had no idea what he looked like. We had never met anyone on my father's side of the family so we had no connection to our grandparents, aunts, uncles or cousins. My mother said that my father had been an only child and both of his parents were already deceased when she met him. The only thing she knew was that he had been born in Philadelphia, PA. It was as if my father had existed alone in the world until he met my mother.

On the day that I saw my father for the first time, Larry, my mother, my brother and I went to the airport to pick him up. I still had not talked to him yet. My mother had made all the initial arrangements for my father to come to Raleigh. We had agreed that we would have this impromptu "family reunion" at my house. We arrived early and sat in the baggage claim area waiting for his plane to arrive. I glanced over at my brother. Sweat was dripping down the side of his face. He kept fidgeting with his hands and picking pieces of imaginary lint from his pants. Strangely, seeing how nervous my brother was made me calmer. I felt a sense of protectiveness come over me and suddenly I was more concerned with my brother's feelings than I was concerned about my own.

I remember sitting there when his plane finally landed waiting in anticipation as each passenger disembarked from the plane. Several passengers emerged and none of them looked like anyone who could possibly be my father. I glanced over at my mother and she did not seem to recognize anyone either. More passengers emerged and still none of them looked close to being my father. Yet again, more passengers came through the gate doors and still no one. Had he changed his mind and backed out at the last minute? Had he decided not to come and meet us? I felt my heart sinking when suddenly my mom stood to her feet and I could tell by the look in her eyes that the last passenger to leave that plane was my father. Larry and I both stood up.

Tears began to well up in my eyes causing my vision to blur. I could feel my husband Larry put his arm around my waist for support. I was standing there crying like a mother looking at her newborn baby for the first time. That's what I felt like as I stood there looking at my father for the very first time that I could remember. I was overwhelmed with emotion. He did look like my brother, or should I say my brother looked like him. My mother was walking towards him and she was smiling from ear to ear. I looked over at my brother; he was crying. My brother was so overwhelmed by his emotions that he couldn't even get up out of his seat and slowly my emotions began to give way to anger.

Suddenly all of the pain and hurt that I had consumed for my father all these years came rushing up inside of me.

"How could this man just walk away from his wife and children all those years ago; how could he walk away from his family?" But he was here now. Wasn't that all that mattered? Didn't he deserve a second chance? If he didn't deserve it I at least owed it to myself to hear what he had to say so I wiped the tears from my eyes and waited for my mother to bring him over to introduce us.

He reached out and shook my hand but he wouldn't look me in the eyes. Instead of shaking his hand I reached out and embraced him in a hug. I sensed that he was a little startled by my reaction because he pulled back from my embrace almost as if my skin was too hot. He seemed slightly uncomfortable. When he realized that I wasn't going to let him go he raised his arms and patted me quickly on the back as if to congratulate me and send me on my way.

He smelled like Old Spice and cigarettes so obviously he was still smoking. His hair was jet black and slicked back with some type of pomade to make it look wavy. He had on a black 3-piece suit with spectator Stacy Adam shoes. He had a tan trench coat draped over his arm. As much as I hated to admit it he looked like a broke down old school player from back in the day. I took a careful look at him and there was no way this man could be fifty-nine. He looked more like he was seventy-nine years old and when I looked beneath his trench coat and saw a cane I knew he was much older than the age he should have been according to my birth certificate.

Something about this man just wasn't right. I was getting strange vibes from him that made the hairs on the back of my neck stand up. For one thing he just looked sneaky; like he was up to no good. When he talked to you he wouldn't really look you in the eyes. Maybe it was a guilty conscious. Let's just say that his reaction to meeting me and my brother had not been like anything that I had expected.

I especially didn't like the way he was looking at my mother. He was definitely glad to see her and he was grinning from ear to ear but there was something about the way he looked at her in his eyes. They looked almost lecherous. Almost like an animal about to devour its prey. He was definitely a different person when he interacted with my mother. He somehow seemed to come alive when he looked at her and talked to her. I had thought that seeing his children, his own flesh and blood, would invoke the same reaction he had towards my mother. Clearly my brother and I did not have the same effect on him that my mother did.

From the time we picked my father up until the time we got to my house my parents were acting like teenage kids smitten with each other. They were holding hands in the back seat of the car, snuggled up close together and whispering. My mom was giggling like some young, love struck teenage girl with a crush on her boyfriend. I had certainly never seen my mother acting like this before and I didn't like it. I mean I wasn't fearful that my father was going to steal my mother's affection away from me or anything like that. I just didn't like the metamorphosis I was seeing transpiring before my eyes. It was as if my father had transformed her into some sort of little silly, giggling adolescent. I could tell she was enamored by him and seemed to be losing all sense of who she really was.

I was a social worker but I had always thought if I could choose another career it would be a detective. I guess I was always leery of people or situations so anytime something did not set right with me in my spirit I would investigate the situation and that was exactly what I set out to do where my father was concerned. I couldn't put my finger on it but something just wasn't right about his story. I know I had questioned him like the Spanish inquisition, but I had thirty-one years' worth of questions bottled up inside and I felt he owed me that much.

I could not remember a time that my intuition had failed me and I wasn't going to be satisfied until I had turned over every stone I could find looking for information about my father. The one question that kept nagging at me was why he had never come looking for us? We never moved from the house I grew up in and as a matter of fact my mother still lives in that house to this day. I could understand that maybe things hadn't worked out between him and my mom, but we were his children. If he had reached out and tried to find us he would have found us still living in the home he had walked away from. He would have found me and my brother sitting right there waiting for him to come back home but he hadn't even bothered to take the time to try to find us. I didn't need him but my brother did.

I guess it's different for boys. I had mama but my brother needed a man to teach him how to be a man. My uncles were there and they stepped right in to take up where my father left off but I guess that wasn't enough for him. For some people I guess that whole "it takes a village to raise a child" works but not for my brother Eddie. He was always searching for something; always wanting more. Maybe because he was named after my father, Steven Edward McNeil, he felt that he had some big name to live up too, except my father hadn't left any shoes to fill because he wasn't there. I remember various times through the years I would ask Eddie if he remembered anything about our father because Eddie was five years old when our father walked out on us. I was always trying to get him to tell me anything he could remember about him but he never wanted to talk about it. He would tell me he didn't remember anything and why was I bringing 'him' up again. That was what we started calling my father; 'him'. I knew Eddie remembered more than he would admit to me because he would always get quiet and get this far away look in his eyes after I mentioned anything about 'him'.

Mama had not been any help either. She would always say, "Child don't you have better things to worry about than 'him'. I didn't dare ask big mama. She had made it known for as long as

I could remember, "Nobody better not even mention 'him' in my house!" Then she would go off muttering things about him under her breath as if no one could hear her but I would always catch a few of her words. "No good, trifling, shiftless…"

I remember one Easter Sunday, I guess I caught mama at the right time because when I asked her about 'him' on this particular day she told me about how she met 'him'. She motioned for me to come and sit beside her on the swing on big mama's porch. I laid my head in her lap and she began stroking my hair. I looked in mama's eyes but I could see that she wasn't really looking at me; she was looking out past the trees as if she had been transcended back in time. Her gaze shifted out towards the horizon and for the first time mama began to tell me about 'him'…

1965

"I was a sophomore in college at Johnson C. Smith

College the first time I met your father. I was com-

ing out of vespers when I heard someone say…

"Excuse me."

"Who, me," I asked, pointing to myself look-

ing around for someone behind me because I

was certain he could not be addressing me.

"Yes you. What's your name?"

He was decked out from head to toe. He was lean-

ing back on the hood of a 1965 Ford Mustang.

"My name is Beverly Jones."

"Hi, Beverly, I am Steven McNeil. Nice to meet you.

You sure are pretty. What's your classification?

"I'm a sophomore and you?"

"I graduated a few years ago. I work here in the city"

"So what are you doing here on campus?"

"I'm looking for my future wife and I think I just found her."

I know I should have run the other way. He was definitely older than I was but there was something exciting and intriguing about him that piqued my interest and instead of turning the other way I walked over to where he was standing. I guess I was impressed with his confidence and boldness.

I must have stayed out there for hours talking to him. In fact I stayed out there so long that he had to drive me back to my dormitory. I just barely missed being late for my curfew. He asked if he could visit me the next Sunday and I told him he could.

I was surprised a couple of days later when someone knocked on my dorm room door and announced that I had a call on the lobby phone. Sure enough it was Steven. Again I was impressed because I had not given him my dorm room number nor had I told him which floor I lived on but somehow he had found me anyway.

Steven came by every Sunday after that; right after assembly. We would drive up to Concord to have dinner. He said he didn't want to interfere with my school work so our once a week date was perfect. I looked forward to the end of assembly every week so I could see Steven.

We had been dating for about six months when I brought him home to meet big mama. She didn't like him from the moment she laid eyes on him. She took me in the back room later that evening and told me not to bring that old man to her house ever again. Big mama had given me money to ride the bus home and I had driven home with Steven instead. I know I should have asked permission to bring him home. I shouldn't have surprised big mama like that but I was so excited for her to meet him. I wanted her to see what I saw in Steven but that wasn't going to happen.

The next time I brought Steven home we were married. Steven and I had eloped. That didn't set well with big mama at all because I still had 2 months left until I graduated from college. My relationship with your father caused a rift between big mama and me but Steven was my husband and he was my family. So, when I graduated from college Steven and I moved to California. We were going to have a fresh start and conquer the world...

Mama got quiet; her gaze still fixed upon the horizon with a distant look in her eyes. She looked down at me and brushed the flyaway hair surrounding my face. She lifted my head from her lap so that she could stand up."

"Now go on girl and play. I gotta go in here and help big mama finish cooking dinner. You stay in the front yard and play. Uncle Jimmy and Uncle Buddy are hiding the Easter eggs in the back yard."

That was the first and last time mama ever talked to me about 'Him' again".

CHAPTER 13

Kandi

The Anger That Lies Within

Repression *[ri-presh-uh n] - To supress the consiousness of pain-ful or disagreeable ideas, memories, feelings, or impulses.*

Kandi was on the board of directors and a volunteer with Me-lina's H.O.P.E. foundation. A couple of months before starting the women's group, Melina had disclosed to Kandi that she commended the way Kandi had been able to get the young teens from H.O.P.E to open up to her during her first mentoring session with them. Melina expressed her desire to have similar results with this group of women.

Kandi had a gift of getting people to open up to her by making them feel at ease. That was part of the reason she had become such a successful lawyer. People trusted Kandi.

Kandi already knew Melina and her niece Tanisha. She was introduced to Susan last year at the H.O.P.E closing ceremony and of course she already knew Naomi. The only woman in the group that she really didn't know yet was Felicia. Even though Kandi could relate to these women because they all had an inherent bond she didn't feel that she really needed to be there. She was just lending moral support to round out the group, however, after hearing Felicia speak, Kandi felt compelled to help her. She also had no choice but to be there after coercing Naomi to join the group with her and that had not been a small task.

Kandi and Naomi had met two years ago when Naomi began working for Mr. Larosa. Mr. Larosa was one of the clients at Kandi's law firm. In fact, Mr. Larosa had been her very first client. He had asked specifically to work with Kandi. She quickly learned that he had a thing for young black women but he always kept their relationship professional and had never crossed the line with her. Mr. Larosa was a smart man and an even shrewder business man. Kandi had let him know in no uncertain terms, without uttering a single word, exactly where she was coming from and he respected that.

Winning her first case for him sealed the deal on their business relationship as well as her professional career. He referred all of his business associates to Kandi's firm with the request that she handle their cases. Mr. Larosa played a big part in her success and subsequently her career path leading to Junior Partner. Of course Kandi put in the work but his business connections landed her some really big cases.

When Kandi first met Naomi she could tell that there was something more than just a business relationship between her and Mr. Larosa. They did an excellent job of covering up their affair but Kandi was a lawyer and it was her job to notice details. Kandi had a very keen eye and often noticed things that others might miss. Kandi knew that the difference between winning a case or losing a case often times came down to the details.

Kandi had to hand it to her though. Naomi knew Mr. Larosa's business almost as well as he did and she had used this knowledge to her advantage, along with a few other things of course. Whenever Kandi was working on a business issue for Mr. Larosa Naomi could be depended upon to supply her with any information or documentation that she needed. Naomi could sometimes find information that even the legal aids in Kandi's firm couldn't find. In fact, Naomi had been right there alongside Kandi many a long night scouring over stacks and stacks of paperwork and legal documents. As a result, they had forged a friendship over the past two years.

"I know that we are all here because we have grown up without our fathers being in our lives", Kandi began to tell the women. "Melina asked me to come here to share my experiences. As we have gotten to know each other a little bit over the past few months I look forward to helping out in any way I can."

"I am here because just like many of you I grew up without my father being present for most of my life. My mother and father got divorced when I was eight and even though he provided for me financially, my father chose not to have anything to do with me after the divorce was final. He remarried a few months later and had another daughter within the same year. He left me and never looked back. He simply moved on with his life; as if I never existed. So I moved on with my life and learned not to depend on my father for anything."

Susan pursed her lips together and shook her head in disapproval. She did not have substantial tolerance for absentee fathers. Kandi understood Susan's reaction. However, contrary to Susan, Kandi had not become bitter.

She no longer had an emotional connection to her father because she had chosen not to dwell on her pain. She had stopped thinking about him a long time ago. As a result, Kandi didn't feel that she really need to be here but Melina had asked her to come. Kandi couldn't refuse because she admired how much Melina devoted her time to her foundation and she was such a caring and giving woman. Kandi would do anything for Melina so she didn't hesitate when Melina asked for her help.

"Let me ask you a question," Melina said to Kandi. "How did it make you feel knowing that your father left you and was raising another family?"

Kandi knew that Melina wanted to delve right in tonight and she knew that she would not be intimidated by Melina's questions but nonetheless the question caught her slightly off guard. It wasn't that the question was too hard to answer. The answer to this question was actually quite simple because she had dealt with it so many times before in the past. It just caught her off guard because she hadn't thought about it in such a long time…

When I was a little girl I thought my father left me because I had done something wrong to make him leave. I thought that I wasn't good enough and that's why he didn't love me anymore. I thought that if I was smarter than anyone else he would love me again. If I was thinner, if I was faster, if I was prettier, if I made the best grades he would be proud of me. As you can imagine the list went on and on. I pushed myself and pushed myself to be the best at everything I did until one day I finally realized that no matter how good or how smart I was it was never going to be enough to bring my dad back home or back into my life so I gave up trying to please him.

As a byproduct of trying to please my dad, I had become a straight "A" student and valedictorian of my graduating class in high school. I had obtained a full four year scholarship to Duke University. I had a bright future ahead of me so I made the decision not to waste all that I had accomplished and decided to be the best I could be for myself and my mom; the one person who had truly been there for me my whole life. Now that I look back over my life I think I did very well for myself, in spite of my father"…

"Were you angry with your father?" Melina asked Kandi.

"No. I was hurt and confused. Back then I felt rejected. I think I was afraid to be angry, if that makes any sense. Then eventually one day I just stopped caring."

"Kandi, it's ok to be angry. Anger is a human emotion. It becomes a problem when we are quick to anger and react impulsively before we have a chance to think about the situation. We also put our emotional health in danger when we dwell on our anger and allow it to fester in our spirit without learning to forgive. Moving on and just ignoring our pain can be mentally unhealthy as well. Simply choosing to overlook or ignore the situation does not mean that the pain is not still there. Many times it is just suppressed and lying dormant waiting to manifest itself. When we allow that to happen it can stagnate and eat away at us like a cancer. Before we know it we have become spiritually and emotionally dead," Melina explained.

Kandi never thought of it that way. Instead she had just tucked her feelings away and decided to forget about them and moved on with her life. She just chose not to address them. But now she could see that pretending they didn't exist was no good either. Emotionally she had killed her father by erasing him from her memory. But now, she could feel the anger and hatred towards her father that she had been suppressing for all of these years starting to rear its ugly head. Kandi realized that maybe she hadn't really "gotten over it". She looked over at Melina and saw that Melina was smiling at her with that knowing glance as if she had read Kandi's mind. All Kandi could do was smile back at her because here she was thinking that she didn't really need to be here and now she knew that this was exactly the place she needed to be.

CHAPTER 14

Felicia

Sisterhood - The Evolution

"Well ladies believe it or not our time is up but before we adjourn I would like to give you a couple of assignments," Melina announced. "First, if you do not already have a journal I would like for you to purchase one. Second, I want you to write a letter to your father. I want you to be brutally honest. Don't over analyze your feelings. Just let it flow. Whatever you feel I want you to write it down in your letter. I want each of you to bring them with you to our next meeting. Don't worry ladies, we are not going to share our letters or read them out loud. So you don't have to be afraid to write down whatever you want because the only person who will ever see what you wrote down is you. This may be very painful for some of you but please trust me. I need you to do this because in order to deal with any problem, issue, pain or hurt you have to first acknowledge it."

Felicia looked down at her watch. It was eight-thirty. She had already missed one and a half hours on her shift and even if she worked as fast as she could she didn't know if she would be able to finish all of her work on time. How would she explain getting home late to Marcus? She simply had no choice. She had to finish on time.

Even though she desperately needed to get started with her work she lingered around Melina's office after the meeting was over until all the other ladies were gone. Felicia felt it was best if they didn't know that she was the "cleaning lady" just yet. When Felicia first joined the group she didn't know who was going to be at the meeting or what type of women they would be so she had made it a point that when she first arrived to work on the days of the meetings to leave her cleaning cart in the break room. She had done this on purpose because she didn't want them to judge her.

Now that they were all gone and the coast was clear she went downstairs to the break room to retrieve her cleaning cart. Felicia had just stepped out of the elevator and was coming down the hallway when she saw the women miraculously standing outside of Melina's office waiting for her. She was stunned to see all of them there. She didn't know what to say or what to do. She felt as if she had just been caught stealing the Mona Lisa or some famous Picasso painting.

"How did you all get back in the building?" she asked them, quite puzzled, because she had clearly seen all of them leave.

"Melina, let us back in," Kandi replied.

Felicia looked back at Melina. She was smiling and rather proud of herself that she had been able to surprise Felicia.

"I saw you constantly looking at your watch when the meeting was over and I realized that you had already missed over an hour on your shift. I know the meeting ran a little bit over schedule tonight and that was my fault. Not to mention that we all stayed around afterwards talking. So I called all the ladies back and let them in the building," Melina explained.

"Called them back for what?" Felicia asked, uncertain of what was going on.

"I called them back so that we can help you finish cleaning the building."

The cat was out of the bag now that Felicia cleaned buildings. Her face and her neck felt flush. She tried to cover her embarrassment by casually replying, "That isn't necessary. I can finish on my own."

"I have no doubt that you can, but I feel guilty that the meeting ran over, so I feel the very least we can do is all chip in and give you a hand," Melina said, still grinning.

In fact, all of the women were smiling at Felicia and they appeared as if they were all eager to help out too. Well, with the exception of Naomi. She wasn't smiling and she didn't strike Felicia as the type to do domestic work, but, she was here so Felicia had to give her credit for that. As much as she had not wanted them to find out what she did for a living just yet, she could really use the help to make sure she finished on time.

Felicia gave each of the ladies instructions for different tasks. Teamwork definitely proved to be an advantage which allowed them to swiftly make up for lost time. Amazingly, they even finished a little early with a few minutes to spare and Felicia was grateful because she would be able to get home on time tonight. She hadn't had to kill herself trying to finish on time and now she didn't have to worry about Marcus.

Some of the ladies looked a little tired after they were done so Felicia really appreciated the sacrifice they had each made to stay here and help her after working all day themselves. She was so used to always doing things by herself that it felt kind of nice to have some help. She didn't have any friends and Marcus kept her alienated from her family. On rare occasions, such as holidays or birthdays they would visit with his family and at one point in time his sister was the only friend she had.

Marcus's sister's nickname was Tiny because she was small in stature. Buy what she lacked in size she made up for in spunk. Tiny was a feisty little woman with the courage of a lion. Even though she didn't know for sure she had a strong inclination about what was going on between Felicia and Marcus and she would always take up for Felicia whenever she was around them. Tiny had a way of making Marcus do things that other people couldn't such as fixing his own plate or getting his own glass of water. She would even cuss him out to his face and tell him about himself. She provoked him and dared him to hit her back. Felicia would be secretly smiling on the inside and silently cheering Tiny on as she talked junk to her brother. Tiny would do all the things Felicia wished she could do; in a way Tiny was her hero.

Felicia knew that Tiny's taunting bothered Marcus but he wouldn't dare say anything to his sister or hit her back and especially not in front of his mother. Tiny meant well and it was her way of getting back at Marcus on Felicia's behalf but in the end it just caused more heartache because Marcus would take his frustration out on Felicia instead. So eventually, Felicia stopped encouraging family visits, aside from Thanksgiving and Christmas. They even stopped talking on the phone as much. Unfortunately, Tiny took Felicia's withdrawal personally and over time they slowly drifted apart.

Felicia missed having a real friend that she could talk to and confide in but now she had hope again. She felt that she had found what she had been searching for, for so long. She knew that she had just met these women but there was a feeling she just couldn't shake. Sometimes there are things that you can't explain, you just know, and this was one of them. Felicia had found a friend, a true friend, in Melina and these women.

Felicia was feeling so good on the drive home after the women's group meeting. She hadn't felt this good in a long time. After being isolated from her family and friends for so long she had forgotten what it felt like to be around other women. It was very sobering to know that she wasn't alone in her problems.

Sometimes when you are going through a situation you feel like you are alone in the world and you are the only person going through your problem. People get so wrapped up in their own personal issues that it becomes difficult to realize that they are not alone. Everyone around us is going through problems. We pass by people every day and never really know what's going on in their lives. Felicia was just grateful that Melina had recognized something going on with her and invited her to join the group. For the first time in a long time Felicia felt hopeful.

Felicia was surprised to find Marcus still up watching television when she walked through the front door; especially on a weeknight. She could feel him watching her when she came in and whenever she became more interesting than the television that could only mean one of two things; either there was about to be a fight or he wanted his needs met. He would have been up out of his chair and in her face by now if he were angry and it only took one look at the grin on his face to confirm what he wanted.

The only time he seemed to smile at her was when he had one thing and one thing only on his mind. Luckily for Felicia she was feeling so good that she didn't even mind having sex with Marcus tonight. She called it sex because it had long since been anything close to making love.

Marcus never quite captured the art of foreplay. When it came to seducing a woman he still possessed the skills of a horny, teenage boy. His skills at pleasing a woman were even worse.

"You seemed pretty relaxed tonight; like your mind was somewhere else, Marcus replied, three minutes later as he rolled off the top of her and lay on his back. "Did something happen at work tonight?"

"No," Felicia lied. "Why do you ask?"

"I don't know there just seemed to be something different. You appeared to be detached or distracted; like your mind was a million miles away while we were making love."

"Making love? Is that what you call it," she thought to herself. She had to stop herself from almost laughing out loud. Felicia had always been detached whenever she had sex with Marcus. But he was right. Tonight was different. For the first time in a long time, if ever, she truly had something else to distract her thoughts while

Marcus got his rocks off. Love had been long gone out of these consummating sessions between her and Marcus. For Felicia it had become nothing more than an arduous chore to assist Marcus in satisfying his sexual desires.

She was simply fulfilling her wifely duties and keeping the peace. She had learned a long time ago how to fake it. She could fake an orgasm with the best of them. In fact, she deserved an academy award for her performance. "And the Oscar goes to, "Felicia Riley", for best performance in faking an orgasm", she thought in her head as she had to stop herself from almost laughing again.

Felicia rolled over onto her side when she was sure that Marcus had fallen asleep. Marcus was right. Her mind had been a million miles away and she couldn't help thinking about Naomi. She admired her for her strength to leave home and put all of her pain behind her at such an early age. There was no way Felicia would have had the courage to do that. For one thing she had her kids to think about. But she knew that she deserved to be happy and she knew there was more to her existence than this misery that had become her life. If only she were as strong as Naomi.

CHAPTER 15

Kandi

A Choice Is Made

Persuasion *[per-swey-zhuh n] - A deep conviction or belief; inducing a belief by appealing to reason or understanding.*

It had been a long day with work and the women's group and Kandi still had to have the conversation with Trent that she had promised him they would have when she got home; three months ago. Trent had been asleep when she got home the last time they were going to have their "talk" and she wasn't about to wake him up to have a conversation with him that she never wanted to have in the first place. She counted it a blessing and decided not to say anything unless he brought it up. Well, he had finally brought it back up and tonight she found Trent wide awake in the den waiting up for her. It was wishful thinking to hope that he had gone to bed early again tonight. She knew better; her good fortune had finally come to an end.

"Hey babe," Kandi replied.

"Hey baby, how was your day?" Trent inquired.

"It was really good. How was your day?" Kandi asked, as she walked over to the couch and gave Trent a kiss.

"My day was good too. I made dinner. Your plate is in the microwave."

"Thanks baby. I'm going to change my clothes first."

Trent was sitting at the kitchen table by the time Kandi came back downstairs. He had warmed her food and put it on the table. He definitely looked ready to talk but Trent was ever the gentleman. He made small talk while Kandi ate her food and he even carried her empty plate over to the sink.

Trent had been very patient with Kandi and she knew she owed him this conversation. She reached out and grabbed Trent's hand, "I know what you're going to ask me."

"Oh you do?" he asked. "What am I going to ask you Kandi?"

"You're going to ask me why I don't want to get married."

"Well, are you ready to give me an answer?"

"Yes," she replied. "Trent, I do want to marry you. I'm just not ready to get married right now. I want to wait until after I make Junior Partner with the firm. We're already living together so for all intents and purposes we're practically married."

"You know I've never liked us living together. That was your idea. The only reason I conceded was to make you happy."

"I know babe and I appreciate you for making that sacrifice but you know how hard I have worked to get where I am today to make Junior Partner. I don't want anything to jeopardize that."

"First of all Kandi, you know that I would never do anything to stand in the way of you fulfilling your dreams. But I honestly don't see how getting married is going to jeopardize you making Junior Partner."

"I know it may sound crazy but I want to become a Junior Partner as Kandi Johnson. You know that I plan to take your surname when we get married but I want to accomplish this goal on my own merit as Kandi Johnson before we get married. Trent you know that I love you and I DO want to be your wife one day."

"I know you love me Kandi and that's why I've waited for you as long as I have. I've excused the missed birthday dinners; both mine and yours, when you forgot to show up. I've seen you work yourself into exhaustion with the late nights and early morning workdays and how many weeks have you pulled sixty to eighty hours in one week? I'm a very patient man Kandi but every man has his limit. I don't know how much longer I can keep waiting but I will keep trying my best to see things your way and understand where you are coming from." Trent stood up and kissed Kandi on the forehead. "I'm tired baby, come on and let's go to bed. You've had a long day and I want to get an early start in the morning"

Turning out the lights along the way Trent grabbed Kandi's hand and led her upstairs to go to bed. She changed out of her clothes and slipped into her night gown. Trent was lying on his side facing towards Kandi with a solemn look on his face when she came out of the bathroom.

"I purposely waited three months to see if you were going to bring up the topic of marriage and you didn't. I know there's more to your hesitation to marry me than you're willing to admit", Trent replied after Kandi had gotten under the covers. "Baby, I'm not your father. I'm nothing like him so when are you going to stop measuring me against the mistakes that he made? I love you. I've been with you through thick and thin and I'm never going to leave you. When you finally understand that, then maybe you'll be ready to get married and realize that it really doesn't matter what your last name is when you make partner. It's the hard work you put in that got you where you are. Not your name."

Trent reached over to turn off the lamp beside the bed. He paused briefly and turned back on his side to face Kandi before adding, "Oh, and one last thing about marriage. You won't ever have to worry about it anymore because I won't ever ask you again."

CHAPTER 16

Susan

The Abscence of Joy

Susan's mind was preoccupied all the way home. Write a letter to her father. She didn't want to write a letter to him. As far as she was concerned he didn't deserve the energy it would take for her to give him any thought. She was done talking to him and could care less about wasting her time writing a letter to him.

Susan didn't like lying but she wasn't ready to tell Larry the truth just yet about the woman's group. Instead she had been telling him that she was working late which wasn't exactly a lie.

She did work a little late in the office; She just omitted telling him that she left the office and attended the group session before she got home. She had never kept any secrets from Larry before but she just wasn't ready to reveal her issues with the whole Julian situation.

It had been months now since Julian had called and they were no closer to the truth than they had been when he first called. Larry had been unsuccessful in reaching Julian's mom Vanessa and she hadn't returned any of his calls. Susan wondered what she trying to hide? Was she trying to hide the fact that she had lied and now she was caught like a trapped animal with nowhere to run? If she was it was all her own fault. No one told her to make up these lies. Didn't she think that one day her son might want to go in search of his father? What was she going to do then? Maybe she hadn't thought things out that far when she was fabricating this scheme way back then and now she was running scared.

Susan didn't know what would possess a woman to do such a thing; to disrupt so many lives and especially the life of her child. She tried putting herself in Vanessa's shoes but she just couldn't fathom the idea. Maybe Vanessa didn't know firsthand the effects of growing up without a father, and then again maybe she did. People react to situations differently and it's all based on their individual points of reference and life experiences. Whether right or wrong Susan chose to believe that Vanessa had done what she felt was right at the time and that's all anyone can do. Susan didn't have all the facts and it wasn't her place to judge Vanessa.

Larry had cooked dinner for the kids and cleaned the kitchen by the time Susan got home. She had already told Larry not to save any food for her because she had leftovers from her lunch at Applebee's. She wasn't ready to face him just yet so she put her things down on the table and turned the kettle on to make herself a cup of hot tea. Thinking through everything on the ride home had made Susan become agitated all over again about the whole situation and she wasn't so sure she would be able to hold it all in.

Larry walked up behind Susan, put his arms around her waist and kissed her on the cheek. "Hey Sweetie, how was your day?" he asked.

"It was a great day," Susan replied.

Larry spun Susan around in his arms eyeing her suspiciously. He wasn't fully buying her joviality. "You don't look like you had such a "great" day and you definitely don't sound like it. What's the matter?"

She should have known better than to try to fool Larry. He knew her like a book. "Nothing is the matter. I did have a great day, I'm just tired. I picked up a new case today, that's why I was working late tonight," Susan replied, telling him the truth. She just omitted a few details again.

"Well, why don't you go on upstairs and run yourself a nice hot bath. The kitchen is cleaned and the kids are in their rooms doing their homework. I'll finish making your tea just the way you like it and then I'll bring it up to you."

"Hi mama," said Danielle as she came traipsing into the kitchen to give her mother a big hug. Susan hugged Danielle back and kissed her on the forehead. "Mama, will you take me to the craft store so I can get some supplies for my language arts project?"

"Baby, your mama is tired I can take you. You should have told me earlier, we could have gone and been back by now," Larry replied to Danielle.

Susan could see the pleading in Danielle's eyes as she looked at her mother. She really wanted Susan to take her. They had missed their bonding time together that day so she didn't mind taking Danielle to the store.

Besides Susan needed a change of scenery and a change of topic to get her mind off of Larry, Vanessa and Julian so, as tired as she was, she actually relished the idea of having an excuse to escape and took Danielle to the craft store. By the time they got back home it was too late for her bubble bath so Susan took a shower instead. She crawled into bed next to Larry and let the soft sounds of his breathing lull her to sleep. Susan was familiar with the old saying "joy comes in the morning" but when the daylight came and she opened her eyes she knew that joy had not come knocking on her door.

CHAPTER 17

Naomi

The Second Seduction

Narcissism *[nahr-suh-siz-em] - Inordinate fascina-*
tion with oneself; excessive self-love; vanity.

N aomi was so deep in thought that it took her a minute to notice the delivery guy standing in front of her desk with a bouquet of 4 dozen yellow and white roses.

Actually, she didn't notice him until he said, "Excuse me ma'am, I have a delivery for a Ms. Naomi Miller."

Naomi instructed him to place the flowers on the corner of her desk as she retrieved her wallet from her purse in order to tip him. His eyes registered surprise and he thanked her profusely when he realized that she had tipped him twenty dollars. Naomi already knew who the flowers were from before she read the card attached to them: "I hope these brighten your day as much as you brighten mine, Warm Regards, Lance".

Naomi was so surprised and excited about the roses that she returned the favor by indulging the delivery guy with a generous tip. Lance had obviously spared no expense on the bouquet so why shouldn't she return the generosity? What surprised her even more was how in the world had Lance discovered that yellow and white roses were her favorite? She thought back to the day he had given her his business card. She had worn her white pencil skirt. The matching blouse she had worn was adorned with a print of white and yellow roses. Very observant; Naomi liked that in a man so she made a mental note to thank him later.

She didn't know how she was going to get through all of the work she needed to get done. Her thoughts had already been lost all morning evaluating the therapy session from the previous night. Now she kept thinking about the best way to thank Lance for the beautiful flowers that were sitting on her desk. To make matters worse, Mr. Larosa kept eyeing the flowers every time he passed by her desk and if she wasn't mistaken she could have sworn that she saw a tinge of jealousy gleaming in his eyes. Of course he didn't say anything which in itself was a sure sign he was jealous.

The session last night with the women had started Naomi reflecting back over her past. She hadn't thought about her life in NY in such a long time. She had tried to erase most of the time she'd spent in NY from her memory. Yet, somehow when she thought back on it now, the memories appeared so fresh and vivid in her mind. In fact she almost felt like she had been morphed backwards in time. She felt as if everything had just happened yesterday; almost as if she was no longer an adult but instead she was that 16 year old kid who had just left home to pursue a better life in NY.

"A penny for your thoughts."

"What?" Naomi replied, slightly startled to see Lance standing in front of her desk because she had not seen him come into the office. She couldn't believe she had done that for the second time that day. That was so unlike her.

"I know that was lame. That was so cliché. It's just that you were so deep in thought you didn't seem to notice that I was standing here," Lance explained.

"Oh, I'm sorry. It's nothing. Well, I just have a lot on my mind lately."

"Is everything ok?" he asked.

"Yes. Everything is fine. This is just our busy season right now and I have a lot of work to do." Naomi was not about to tell Lance the real reasons why she had been distracted. Instead she smiled at him and replied, "So what brings you by the office?"

"I'm here to see you beautiful lady. I was hoping to take you to lunch but now I'm not so sure since you're so busy. I guess I'll have to get a rain check."

"Lance I would love to go to lunch with you but I really am swamped. How about a rain check for dinner tonight," Naomi asked? She needed to work through lunch since she hadn't gotten very much accomplished all morning long. Her mind had been elsewhere.

"I can't make it tonight. I have a working dinner meeting."

"Are you sure? I would really like to thank you properly for the roses you sent me today," she added for extra emphasis.

"So you liked them?"

"They're beautiful. What's not to like?"

Naomi could see the wheels spinning in Lance's head as he replied, "How about meeting me after my business meeting for an after dinner drink and dessert?"

"Deal," she replied.

"Why don't you come by the restaurant at 9:00," Lance instructed as he bent down and kissed her goodbye on the cheek before turning to leave.

As Naomi turned back to her computer she became keenly aware that Mr. Larosa was staring at her. He was clearly agitated with her and she had never seen this side of him before. She wasn't sure how long he had been watching her exchange with Lance but now she was more convinced than ever that gleam in his eyes was jealousy.

On her first date with Lance, Naomi had worn her sexy red dress and he hadn't taken the bait. Naomi thought perhaps Lance preferred the subtle approach and there was absolutely nothing subtle about her red dress. That dress had one purpose in mind and there was no doubt as to what that purpose was. Albeit, it didn't fulfill its purpose the first night she had gone out with Lance but it definitely turned some heads so she knew it wasn't the dress.

Tonight she was going to try a more subtle approach by wearing her little black dress. It was still sexy but it also had a level of sophistication and elegance. It had never failed her yet and she knew it wouldn't fail her tonight.

Naomi arrived a little early and took a seat at the bar. That allowed her to have a vantage point to watch Lance discreetly. His business guests were definitely enthralled in the conversation. They seemed to be hanging on his every word. Lance exuded a style and confidence that only heightened his sexuality. She loved a strong, take charge, confident man and Lance was definitely commanding attention.

Naomi felt someone sidle up beside her and whisper in her ear, "Hello beautiful." One whiff of the expensive cologne and she knew immediately that it was Lance. She had seen him excuse himself from the table a few minutes ago after he had paid the bill and the meeting appeared to be over but she just assumed he was going to the restroom. She had no idea that he had spotted her so she was caught completely off guard; so much for being discreet.

Lance escorted her back to his table and introduced her to his dinner guests. They all stood up as Lance offered Naomi his chair. Most of the men were prominent business men and leaders in the community. She even recognized a few of them as business associates of Mr. Larosa. In the manner of some unspoken, secret code of manly ethics, they all remained standing and bid their farewells so that Lance and Naomi could be alone.

Whatever the reason she was glad to finally have Lance all to herself. She opted for coffee and dessert instead of an after dinner drink while Lance ordered a glass of cognac. She was definitely fascinated with Lance and had to remind herself that she was trying the subtle approach this time. They were having a great time and great conversation, so Naomi waited until what she felt was the appropriate amount of time before she suggested that they continue the rest of their evening back at her place.

She couldn't believe what happened next. Lance turned her down. She was in such a state of shock that she could barely comprehend what was happening. Lance was yawning and saying something about how exhausted he was. It had been a long day and he had to get up early the next morning to finalize the details of the meeting he had just had that evening. Everything else he said after that might as well have been blah, blah, blah because that was all she heard.

Lance signaled the waitress for the check. He walked her to her car, kissed her on the cheek, and waved goodbye. She was stunned and speechless to now find herself on the freeway headed home. Alone!

This was the second time that Lance had thwarted her advances. Was she slipping that bad? No, it definitely wasn't her. Naomi found herself wondering, "Was Lance gay or was he married?" She ruled out all thoughts of him being gay. "So could he be married? " He wasn't wearing a wedding ring but that didn't necessarily mean he wasn't married. Plenty of married men don't wear wedding rings. Besides he had given Naomi his phone number on the back of his business card and when she called him he told her that it was his personal number. "Did he have a separate number that he kept private from his wife? " He had even said, "I handle all of my personal affairs directly." Naomi had just assumed he meant that he handled his personal business himself. She hadn't taken him literally to mean marital affairs.

Naomi was confused though, because he didn't behave like a man who was having an affair. It wasn't as if they had met in some secluded, out of the way place a hundred miles from Raleigh. In fact, he had invited her to his restaurant on their first date and he had pulled out all the stops. Lance's demeanor and presence alone commanded attention not to mention the fact that his face had been plastered all over the newspaper and the local news when his restaurant first opened. He had been a professional athlete so almost everyone knew who he was. Naomi doubted he would have brought her to his restaurant if he had not wanted to be seen. Even with all of his accolades he had never struck her as the arrogant type who would be bold and brazen enough to flaunt an affair for everyone to see. In fact, he didn't strike her as the type of man to belittle his wife by having an affair.

Naomi didn't know why she was making such a big deal out of this because she always dated married men so what difference did it make if Lance was married or not? The difference was she was falling for Lance and she had never fallen for a man like that before in her life. If she didn't know better she would have bet that he was using the classic ploy of playing hard to get? Well, if he was it was working because he was driving her crazy.

She almost had to laugh at the irony of it all. Lance was driving her crazy and she was going to group therapy sessions. Well, Naomi was definitely looking forward to the therapy session that week because she had a lot to talk about.

CHAPTER 18

Kandi

Decisions

Fixation *[fik-sey-shuh n] - A preoccupation with*
one subject, issue, thing, etc.; obsession.

Kandi couldn't get their conversation off her mind as she drove to the group meeting. It had been bothering her for weeks now. She hadn't given Trent the answer he was looking for. To Trent, things couldn't be any simpler or clearer: if you loved someone, you got married. In his mind, it was as simple as that.

Trent came from a small town and a very well educated family. His parents had met in college and married as well as had his grandparents. Both of his parents had become lawyers and ran a well-established law firm in his hometown. His grandfather had been the principal of the local African American High School and his grandmother and been an elementary school teacher so his family was very well known and respected in the community.

His parents had been married for 35 years so it was only natural that he wanted a wife, kids and the experience of raising a family in a small town like he had grown up in. Before he met Kandi it had been his intention to return home and run for the office of district attorney after practicing law for a few years in his family's law firm. He had goals and dreams too so he knew how important Kandi's dreams were to her. He just didn't know that it meant everything to her at all costs; even if that cost meant losing him. That's what hurt him so much. That her determination to prove herself to her father meant more to her than he did and that's what deflated his spirit regarding their relationship.

Kandi knew that Trent felt dejected. She also knew that he meant every word of what he had said. He was a patient man. In fact he had the patience of Job, but he was telling the truth. He wouldn't ask her again.

Equally as disturbing to Kandi was Trent's implication that she was comparing him to her father. Had she been subconsciously comparing Trent to her father? Was she really afraid of a real commitment with Trent because she had been afraid that he would leave her the same way that her father had left her mother?

Kandi's hesitation to get married didn't really make sense to Trent but he respected her reasons for wanting to wait a little while longer and she loved him even more for his patience with her. She was truly blessed to have such a great man but at the same time she was afraid that Trent was on the verge of giving up. She had backed him in a corner with very little options and she needed to share her fears and concerns with the women…

"I think I may have really messed up this time. I may have gone too far and pushed Trent to the edge."

What do you mean Kandi," Melina asked her?

"I know that I have told you all about him and what a wonderful man he is but what I haven't mentioned is the issue we've been having. I never said anything before now because we've all been focused on our relationships with our fathers. But he said some things to me a few weeks ago that I just can't get off my mind. He accused me of comparing him to my father."

"Well you know Kandi, sometimes other people can have valid observations about us that we may not see or want to acknowledge about ourselves," Melina explained. "So, do you think there is any validity in what he said?"

"No. I honestly know that Trent is nothing like my father and he would never leave me nor would he ever abandon his children."

"Hmm, are you so sure about that," Susan remarked sarcastically? "I'm sorry, I didn't mean that," Susan apologized when everyone turned to look in her direction.

"Then why are you so worried?" Melina continued questioning Kandi.

"It's just that he wants to get married and I want to wait until I reach one of my career goals. He's my best friend and I'm afraid I might lose him if I continue to ask him to wait," Kandi replied.

"Well, let me ask you this. What are you more afraid of Kandi? That you might lose him or you might not reach the goals that you have set for yourself?" Melina asked.

"Honestly, I'm more afraid of not reaching the goals that I have set for myself. It's like something I can't control and that's what scares me. I won't allow myself to bend. I can't bend because that's who I am."

"What is wrong with you?," Felicia replied "You do realize that you have a good man don't you? Do you know how many women would snatch him up in the blink of an eye?

"I never said that Trent was not a good man. I am fully aware of what a good man I have but I'm still not ready to rush into marriage," explained Kandi.

"Rush into marriage?" Felicia asked rhetorically, rolling her eyes up to the ceiling. "Didn't you say that you have been dating for about six years?"

"Look I already get this at home. I don't need this grief from you too," Kandi replied defensively.

"Kandi is right," Melina interjected. "Ladies let's remember that this is the no judgment zone."

"I'm sorry," Felicia replied, softening her tone as she apologized to Kandi. "It's just that Trent sounds too good to be true and it seems like you are about to let a good man slip right through your fingers. I didn't mean to sound judgmental towards you. I just want to make sure that you realize what you have before it's too late."

Kandi couldn't help but glance over at Naomi because Naomi had been telling her the same thing for as long as she could remember but it was different now that her business was out in the open for everyone else to see. Somehow it sounded more valid coming from Felicia. Perhaps it was different because it was coming from the perspective of someone who didn't know her as well as Naomi did. There was an air of innocence about the comments coming from a new acquaintance that somehow made the words resonate with more truth.

Breaking the silence in the room, Melina offered words of encouragement saying, "Kandi, in the last session, I know you said that you grew up always trying to do your best to please your dad and eventually you gave up trying but I think the compulsion to succeed is still there. I think that's why you can't compromise with Trent on this issue. However, the good news is that you can learn to overcome this behavior and I can help you. We are all here to help you and to support you."

CHAPTER 19

Naomi

City of Broken Dreams

//Melina, if it's alright with you and the rest of the group, I'd like to go next," Naomi said, looking around the room at everyone. Melina nodded her head in agreement along with the other women so Naomi began to share the truth about her life in NY…

"It has been a long, long time since I've thought about my past but ever since the first week we met that seems to be all I can think about. I know you never really ever forget about your past but somehow your life moves on and in the process you just stop thinking about it until something triggers the memories to shift into the forefront of your mind. I guess that's what happened since I started coming to these meetings. I started thinking about what happened to me in NY.

When I first arrived in NY I admit I was scared but I was also excited at the same time if that makes any sense. Everything was falling into place just as I had planned. I had my apartment, I had secured a job, school was starting in the fall; life was good.

I had been in NY a little over a month. On this particular day I had just finished working my shift and took the subway as I normally did. I had one stop to make before I got home so I got off a couple of blocks from my house. The station was pretty deserted but I didn't think anything of it until out of nowhere this guy steps out from around a column and stops dead in front of me pointing a gun in my face.

I couldn't believe this was happening to me. This had to be a joke, but no one else was around and he wasn't laughing. He demanded that I give him my purse. I hesitated and grabbed the strap, clutching it closer to my body. I looked behind me but there was nowhere to run. I couldn't believe that no one else had gotten off on this stop. I guess I hesitated too long because he grabbed my purse so forcefully that I fell to the ground and he snatched it off my shoulder as I was lying flat on my back on the ground.

He started running up the subway steps so I collected my wits about me and my survival skills quickly kicked in. I took chase after him. I knew he had a gun and I didn't know what I would do if I caught up to him but I had to do something. I had to get my purse back because my entire life savings was in there. By the time I reached the top of the stairs he had already disappeared into the crowd and I had no idea which direction he had taken. I looked around frantically in all directions for any glimpse of him but he was nowhere in sight. It was as if he had just vanished into thin air.

Suddenly an overwhelming sense of dread washed over me when the reality began to sink in that all the money I had worked for and saved all those years was gone. I knew it wasn't safe to carry around that much cash money. I had known for a while that I needed to open a bank account. The ironic part about the whole situation is; I was on my way to the bank that very moment I got off the subway with all the money I owned in the world and in the blink of any eye it was gone, just like that.

I felt like a crazy woman just standing there looking around in circles not knowing what to do next. The thing about NY though, is no one even seemed to notice me standing there. The city that never sleeps kept moving past me without skipping a beat. Part of me wanted to cry and part of me was too shocked with disbelief over what had just happened. In my opinion crying never solved anything so I wouldn't let myself succumb to the tears I could feel welling up in my eyes. Although it felt like it in that moment, deep down inside I knew that it wasn't the end of the world. I had to focus on the positive and I had to think of a way out of my situation.

As the adrenaline rush was wearing off and the reality of what had just happened began to set in I noticed my hands were shaking. Suddenly I realized that I had no one to run home too. No one to wrap their arms around me and tell me everything was going to be alright. I had no mama to run home too to soothe away my fears; not that she would have anyway. I had made the decision to leave home and now here I was, all alone in the real world.

I turned around and started walking in the opposite direction of the bank; towards home. The fresh air would help me clear my head and I needed time to think. I was too terrified to go back to the subway. Despite the fact that no one had come to my rescue, somehow I felt safer up on the streets with the people of New York then all alone down on the subway platform.

Thank God, I had paid my first month's rent and my last month's rent as a security deposit when I first moved in but I didn't have a signed lease. I couldn't think about that now. All I could do was take one day at a time and right now I still had twenty two days left on my second month's rent payment that I had paid. If only I had paid up all of my rent for the year directly to the landlord, instead of putting the money in the bank, none of this would be happening right now.

At least I had twenty two days to figure out how I was going to come up with next month's rent. Technically I could probably get a few more days before my landlord could evict me out of my apartment but I wanted to try everything I could do to avoid getting evicted. I had known that it could be risky renting an apartment without a lease but then I started to look on the bright side and I realized that maybe this time it may have worked out in my favor; I wasn't bound to this apartment by a lease. Another plus in my favor was the fact that there had been no credit check done so if I had to bounce from this apartment it wouldn't go against my credit. But this was another detail that I couldn't worry about right now.

Somehow I had to get more money but all I could think to do at this point in time was to work more hours, try to find another job and pray for a miracle. So, as the young people say today, I started to get my grind on. Initially I began working more hours by volunteering to work double shifts when someone called out sick or couldn't work their shift. I assisted the bus boys with cleaning up the tables in my section so that people waiting could be seated faster. I figured the more people that could be seated in my area the more opportunity for tips. I also revved up my customer service skills into overdrive. I could have been the poster child for customer service. It was working too. My tips had more than doubled and with the extra hours I had enough for rent but I still would need money for food and money for transportation to get back and forth to work.

I could eat at the diner and I could walk to work in the morning to save some money but as crazy as this may sound considering my recent robbery, it was safer for me to take the subway home at night. Then there was the issue of school. I had already signed up to take my GED course at Medgar Evers College. I didn't know what I was going to do once school started because I wouldn't be able to work as many hours. But as before, all I could do was take one day at a time and for the time being it appeared as if I would at least be able to make my third month's rent.

When I arrived at work the next day Mr. Davis, the owner of the diner, called me into the office. I could feel the palms of my hands begin to sweat. I looked around the kitchen to see if anyone else had been summoned to the office; nope, no one else, just me. My heart was racing. I took a deep breath and ran my hands up and down the sides of my pants to remove the excess moisture before taking a seat on the other side of the desk facing Mr. Davis.

"Naomi, I've been getting a lot of feedback about you from our customers and it has me a little concerned."

I felt a bead of sweat pop up on my forehead. Suddenly my mouth felt as dry as cotton. This wasn't making any sense to me. I had been busting my behind for the past several weeks. Going out of my way to make sure my customers were taken care of, working extra shifts. Was I about to get fired? I couldn't afford to lose this job. My very life depended on it. I felt like I was standing in that subway all over again with a gun pointed directly in my face.

I almost didn't recognize my own voice when I began speaking in a whisper to Mr. Davis. Barely audible, I managed to say, "I don't understand. I've been working so hard. I've worked double shifts, I've volunteered to work when other people couldn't work their own shift, I've helped bus tables, and no matter how tired I've been I have never let it affect the service I give to my customers."

"I know and that's what has me concerned. How in the world am I going to get customers to come to our new location if you are working over here and how are we going to keep our current customers here if I move you over to the new location?"

"M-move me, other location…Mr. Davis, I'm confused. What are you talking about?"

"I'm opening up a second diner location a few blocks from here. I've noticed your hard work over the past few weeks and I've also gotten numerous compliments from customers regarding your customer service. So, I would like for you to move over to the new location and be my head waitress. You'll still get tips but I'm also giving you a raise on your base pay," Mr. Davis explained.

Was this really happening? Was I getting a raise? This was great news so why wasn't I jumping up to shake Mr. Davis' hand and thanking him profusely? Instead, my mind was racing with questions. I was grateful, don't get me wrong but I didn't have a customer base at the new diner and there were no guarantees about how well business would pick up at the new location.

"Is everything ok Naomi? I thought this would be great news"

How could I ask for anything more when Mr. Davis was already being so generous?

"It is great news Mr. Davis", I managed to smile. "I am very grateful for this opportunity, it's just I'm not sure that I will be able to make the same amount of money at the new location as I make right now. I'll have to rebuild my customer base. Mr. Davis I need to make the same amount of money I am making right now. Unfortunately I can't afford to take a pay cut right now. I'm sorry."

"I see", replied Mr. Davis. He sat there in silence for a moment with his eyebrows furrowed together in a frown, tugging at the hairs on his chin before he began speaking again. All of a sudden he sat up, tall in his seat, and leaned towards me. He was smiling as if he had just discovered some great new invention. "Well what about this, I know you have been working a lot of double shifts lately. Would you be able or willing to work in both locations?"

This was definitely too good to be true. Unable to contain my excitement any further I reached out and grabbed Mr. Davis hand in a firm handshake.

"Yes I can. Well at least I can for a while. I'm planning to start school in September, but until then I'll work as many hours as I can. Thank you Mr. Davis. Thank you so much for this opportunity. I promise you I won't let you down. I promise."

"I'm sure you won't Naomi, I'm sure you won't."

I loved working at the new diner. It was amazing how much of a change there was in the clientele between the two locations. We were still in the same general vicinity; the buildings were within mere blocks of one another. I didn't have nearly as many customers at the new diner but the tips were sometimes almost double the amount at the new location which more than made up for the difference in the volume of customers. I was bringing in some serious money! Things were finally beginning to look up for me since the robbery…or so I thought.

I was on my way home one afternoon after a couple of weeks working at the new diner to take a break for a few of hours in between shifts. As I got closer to the brownstone I saw several police cars in front of my building and a few of my neighbors standing outside pleading with the police. The lady who lived in the apartment below me was sitting on the stoop. Her shoulders were slightly humped over. Her hands were covering her face and her body was swaying back and forth from side to side. She was visibly shivering and as I got closer to the building I could hear her crying.

There were no fire trucks and there were no flames coming out the building so it couldn't be on fire. Was someone hurt? I looked around and there were no ambulance or EMT personnel there either. So what was going on? That all too familiar feeling of dread that I seemed to be so acquainted with lately came over me. No one had to tell me that the police were not here to give us any good news. All I had to do was look around at my neighbors.

I sat down on the opposite stoop from the lady in the downstairs apartment. How could I keep taking one step forward to only turn around and take two steps back? Now I understood why she was crying and my other neighbors were pleading with the police. They were asking questions that no one seemed to have the answers to.

We were being evicted. Evicted! I had been breaking my back, working overtime, working double shifts, working two jobs to pay my rent after all my money was stolen and I was being evicted anyway? Although it hadn't made sense when I first moved in, everything started to make sense know. Now I understood why Mr. Richardson never required a security deposit, never required a credit check or never required a lease.

What I discovered that evening, besides the fact that I was now homeless, was that Mr. Richardson had received special funding from the City of NY as part of a city re-vitalization project. We found out that by receiving funds from the program, Mr. Richardson was required by city code to obtain permits and make necessary repairs to bring the building up to code. He was also required to pay taxes which he had failed to do, however, the primary reason we were being evicted was because the property was being foreclosed by the bank. Needless to say, Mr. Richardson had not been paying on his loan either. He had collected special revitalization funding from the city, a loan from the bank, and he had been collecting rent money doing only God knows what with all that money. I had been robbed again.

I had less than an hour to get all of my belongings out of the building before the police were going to put a pad lock on it. I also had less than three hours before I was supposed to start my second shift at the new diner. I couldn't show up at work with everything I owned strapped to my back. I decided that I would at least find an affordable motel room for a couple of nights until I could think of my next move. I still didn't have a bank account but nowadays I kept all of my money strapped to my body, neatly concealed under my clothes. I wasn't going to get jacked again. They would have to kill me to get my money this time and if they did, it wouldn't really matter because I would be dead.

I chose a hotel several blocks away from the diner. It meant a longer commute to work but I didn't want to take any chances of running into anyone from work. I couldn't afford for anyone to know I didn't have a place to live.

Based on the daily motel rate I expected this place to be pretty bad but I wasn't quite prepared for what greeted me when I turned the key and opened the door to enter the room. I grew up with very humble surroundings but this place left a lot to be desired. The décor of the room had not been updated in at least two or three decades. The bed spread looked like it had seen better days. It was covered with lint balls undoubtedly showing its age.

The room was raunchy to say the least. The smell of pine sol trying to mask the overwhelming smell of stale, musty air was enough to be sickening. To make matters worse the air conditioner had been turned off which made the room stuffy and humid.

However, in spite of my current situation and everything that had happened I decided that instead of dwelling on the negative I would suck it up and focus on the positive. I had a place to lay my head, I wasn't on the street and for now I was safe. One day at a time is all I could worry about for now. At least for the next couple of nights I knew where I would lay my head and I needed to get back to work for my second shift.

I truly dreaded going to the motel that night after work. I ate my dinner at the diner because I was afraid of what might crawl out of the woodwork if I brought any food into the room. It was a roach motel to say the least. I took my shower, lined the bed spread with plastic garbage bags I had managed to take from the diner and slept in my clothes. The rustling of plastic underneath my head kept me awake for hours until fatigue consumed me and eventually I fell asleep.

The following morning I got up and I put a smile on my face. From the outside looking in, no one knew that my world was crumbling around me. In the mean time I decided to fake it until I could make it. I didn't know how long I was going to be able to keep up the charade but I had to try.

As usual, I arrived at work the next morning at four forty-five and waited for Slim to unlock the diner. I always arrived before him. If I had a key I wouldn't have to stand outside waiting every day for him to let me in. I could start prepping all the stations and we also wouldn't have to rush every morning to get the diner ready because Slim was late. I wouldn't have to keep walking up and down the block either so no one would see me all alone standing outside the diner waiting. It was plain and simple; I needed a key to the diner.

That was it! How could the solution to my problems be that simple? If I had a key I could come back to the diner at night after it closed and I could sleep in one of the booth seats; at least until I could figure something else out. It was better than sleeping in my clothes at the hotel on top of plastic garbage bags; afraid to close my eyes for too long.

I knew Mr. Davis liked me and had entrusted me with more responsibilities but I didn't know if he trusted me enough to give me a key. Maybe if he knew how long I had to wait every morning

I NEVER DANCED WITH MY FATHER | 129

for Slim to open the diner he would give me a key. I didn't want to get Slim in trouble but I was desperate and someway, somehow I had to get a key to that diner. The best way I knew how was to play on Mr. Davis's sympathy so I turned on the charm and sashayed into his office between the breakfast and lunch rush while the diner was a little less busy.

"Hi, Mr. Davis. How are you today," I inquired?

"There she is, my star employee," Mr. Davis replied, causing me to blush. "I'm fine; what brings you into my office," motioning for me to take a seat?

"I wanted to thank you again for everything you have done for me. It means a lot to me to know that I have your confidence and trust."

"Naomi you are my favorite employee and you have earned my trust and appreciation by your dedication and hard work. It takes a lot to earn my respect."

"Thank you," I replied, blushing again.

"I get the sense that there's something more."

Was I that obvious? I was trying my best to be as transparent as I could but I guess Mr. Davis knew me better than I thought he did.

"I know this is a huge request but I was wondering if there was any way that I could possibly get a key to open up the Diner for the mornings that I work over here?"

"Slim has a key to open the diner. Is there a problem?"

"Well, it's just that I always get here first; before Slim. I just don't feel safe all alone that early in the morning waiting by myself."

"How long do you have to wait on Slim every day?"

"Not too long," I replied, hoping my answer would be enough to satisfy Mr. Davis.

"Naomi, how long?"

I lowered my head before replying, "Forty-five minutes to an hour. If I wait for the next train then I'll be late. Look Mr. Davis, I'm not telling you this to get Slim in trouble. I'm only trying to get a key, so I can be safe. Please, don't say anything to Slim," I begged Mr. Davis, reaching across his desk to touch his hand.

"I'll just have to come down and let you in," he smiled and patted my hand reassuringly.

"No, that's way too early for you to have to come all the way here just to unlock the door to let me in. Then what will you do while Slim and I are preparing the diner for breakfast. Please don't take this the wrong way but you would just be in our way and probably slow us down. Slim and I have a system and we work well together."

"Well, Slim does seem to have an affinity towards you and there is no way I can have you standing outside that long every day. It's just not safe and pretty soon it will be too cold, you'll freeze. Let me see what I can do about getting some keys made and I'll have them for you before your shift ends today."

I knew Mr. Davis wasn't too pleased with the news that Slim arrived nearly an hour late every day but he also knew that he would be hard pressed to find anyone else as loyal or hard working as Slim. Everyone knew that it was Slim's cooking that had kept customers coming back to the diner time and time again; some of them every day. Right now I was going to get a key and that was all that mattered to me. I felt like I had just won a million dollars. One of my problems had been solved and now I had to figure out what to do about the other one…

CHAPTER 20

Tanisha

Always At A Distance

Psychosomatic *[sahy-koh-suh-mat-ik] - Relationship between the mind and the body in which symptoms can be
brought on my the mind instead of the physical body.*

Jordan, Tanisha's roommate, looked up from her computer when
Tanisha walked into the dorm room they shared.

"So, how did your session go tonight? Did the ladies reveal
any juicy secrets," Jordan laughed.

"No, and I couldn't tell you what we discussed if I wanted to.
You are a psychology major too and you are fully aware of what

doctor-patient confidentiality means," Tanisha replied. She didn't mean to sound rude but it had been a long day and she was tired.

"Yes, I am aware of what doctor-patient confidentially means," Jordan replied sarcastically. "But can't you tell me a little something? You don't have to mention any names. It's not like I know who they are and what are the odds that I would ever run into any of these women again in life?"

"This world is smaller than you think," Tanisha replied.

"How long have we known each other?"

"10 years. And your point is?"

"You still don't trust me do you," Jordan replied, shaking her head. Jordan was hurt and offended that Tanisha didn't trust her.

"Of course I trust you."

"That's not what I mean," Jordan replied.

"So you're going to try to guilt me into telling you what went on at the women's session. Is that what you mean?" Tanisha asked.

"I mean deep down inside you really don't trust me. Well I trust you and doctor-patient privilege aside, I would tell you what happened in those sessions because I trust you THAT much to keep anything I tell you in confidence. But obviously the feeling is not mutual."

"Look Jordan, I would tell you but I just want to make sure that I am doing everything by the book because I don't want to let my Aunt Melina down. She's helping me out and you know how much this means to me. What? Don't look at me like that. I do trust you Jordan."

"Yeah, like you trusted Xavier, Rhonda, Cassandra, Jamaal. Should I go on?"

"No. You know how hard it is for me to trust people and I had good reasons not to trust them."

"No you didn't. You never gave any one of them a chance. You shut them down without ever really getting to know them."

"Can we just change the subject please?"

"Struck a nerve huh, didn't I? Well, the truth hurts sometimes Tanisha and whether we like it or not, the truth is the truth."

Jordan was right, but as much as Tanisha loved her like a sister and wanted to trust her completely she couldn't. It was just too hard.

Jordan knew Tanisha better than anyone. They met when Jordan's family moved into the house across the street the summer before they both started middle school. Tanisha could still vividly remember the first day they had met. She was sitting on her bed reading a book when she heard the sound of a large truck coming down the street, which was rather unusual for their neighborhood. She rushed over to the window and stood with her back against the wall peeping out of the side of the curtain to see what was going on. Tanisha saw a huge tractor trailer sitting in front of the house across the street with its engine idling. It seemed like it had taken forever for that house to sell but now an eighteen wheeler moving van was parked there.

As Tanisha was still standing there peeking out of the window a minivan came around the corner and pulled up right behind the moving truck with Jordan's family inside. Jordan got out of her car and sticking out from the top of her backpack was an "American Girls" doll named Addie. Tanisha glanced over to her bed where her own Addie doll was lying; surrounded by all of Tanisha's other stuffed animals. Even though she hadn't played with Addie in years, she still kept her doll lying on her bed. Addie had become more of a keepsake and was one of Tanisha's most prized possessions. Tanisha immediately knew that she and Jordan were destined to be friends because they had something in common; they both had Addie "American Girl" dolls.

Tanisha continued watching the family for a few more minutes before rushing downstairs to tell her mother about the new family moving in across the street. She asked her mother if she could go over to introduce herself and welcome the new family to the neighborhood. Tanisha's mother told her to give them time to get settled and they would all go over and introduce themselves as a family. Tanisha asked her mom every day that week on the way home from summer camp if they could go meet the new neighbors and every day her mother gave her the same reply, "No, not today. Let's give them more time to get settled."

On the following Saturday morning, after the breakfast dishes were cleared, Tanisha's mom started making her famous banana pudding. Everyone loved her banana pudding because she made it from scratch. She used the recipe on the side of the box of Nabisco Vanilla Wafers with a few of her own little secret touches. None of that banana flavored instant pudding mix for Tanisha's mom. She would always buy two boxes of vanilla wafers because she liked to put extra wafers in it. In fact, it was more like vanilla wafer pudding than banana pudding. She even went through the trouble of topping it off with an old fashioned egg white meringue topping, browned to perfection in the oven to form an appetizing golden brown hue.

If Tanisha's mom was making her banana pudding, that could only mean one thing. Today was the day that they were going to meet the new neighbors. This was her signature "new neighbor" welcome dish and also her way of extending southern hospitality.

Jordan and Tanisha soon became inseparable and they went everywhere together. Jordan would come over to Tanisha's house and they would stay in Tanisha's room talking for hours. Their mothers would often say they couldn't imagine what the two girls had to discuss for so long but somehow they never seemed to run out of things to talk about. If Jordan came over to Tanisha's house, Tanisha would walk her to the end of her driveway and wait until Jordan crossed the street to the end of her own driveway. They would say goodnight then turn to wave one final good bye once they had stepped inside of the doorway of their respective homes. If Tanisha were at Jordan's house they would do the same, only Jordan would walk Tanisha to the end of her driveway and wait until Tanisha had crossed the street to her own driveway.

Tanisha even got Jordan a job as a junior camp counselor at her Church's summer youth camp. Of course they didn't get paid but it was a great experience and it made them feel important to be able to boss the younger kids around a little bit. They both had two younger brothers who were the same ages so it was no surprise that Jordan and Tanisha became like sisters.

However, as close as Jordan and Tanisha became, Tanisha still kept a small place in her heart distant. It wasn't just Jordan. It was a place that Tanisha refused to let anyone get close to.

Jordan was the only one true friend that Tanisha had and that was by choice. Tanisha had lots of friends and was very popular in school. But despite her popularity and the number of friends she had, Tanisha chose to only allow her other friends to become associates to her. Deep down inside Tanisha knew why but she had never let anyone else know why; not even Jordan. Everyone else believed that she was ok. That was why she was studying psychology. She wanted to help other people like her Aunt Melina did but she also wanted to find the answers that she was trying to discover about herself.

Tanisha knew that Jordan's feelings were hurt. Jordan wasn't giving Tanisha the silent treatment but she had shut down. Tanisha hadn't meant to hurt her feelings. But Jordan was right; Tanisha didn't allow anyone to get close to her.

Tanisha was going to apologize but she decided against it because with an apology Jordan would expect her to reveal something about the session and Tanisha wasn't going to so she just left well enough alone. Tanisha needed to study for a test so she used Jordan's silent treatment to her advantage. She would find a way to apologize to Jordan a few days later when she knew that Jordan would no longer pressure her into telling her about the meeting and she was no longer feeling hurt.

CHAPTER 21

Susan

The Lies We Tell

Susan pulled into the parking lot of Melina's building and parked next to Kandi. Kandi was applying lipstick so Susan looked in the rear view mirror and decided to freshen up hers as well. They walked into the building together and made small talk until they reached Melina's office. Susan always loved the peacefulness and pleasant aroma that greeted them as they entered into Melina's office.

Susan couldn't believe that they had only been meeting for over six months now. It felt like they had already known each other for years. In the beginning Susan had honestly been a little reluctant to attend the women's group and now she looked so forward to it that she wished they could meet every week instead of every other week.

They had established a pattern of taking turns going first and this week it was Susan's turn to start. After Melina prayed Susan resumed where she had left off from the last session and continued telling the women about her father…

I remember so many times growing up wondering if my dad was still alive or not; hoping that I could just have one chance to talk to him", Susan began. "I guess I was searching for something, anything, to hold on to that would give me a glimpse of who I was. I never felt quite complete, like half of me was missing. I wanted to know where I came from; who was this other person who had made me.

I always hated filling out new patient forms at the doctor's office where you were required to fill out your family health history because I only knew the information from one side of my family. I had no idea what medical issues that I could have inherited from my father because I didn't know anything about him. Now was my chance.

I had so many questions as I watched my mother and father sitting together at my kitchen table while I made all of us some tea. They were idly chatting with my brother sitting close by, who was obviously engrossed in their conversation because he didn't hear me when I asked him to get the half and half out of the fridge. As I walked over to the table carrying the cups of tea, I discovered that my father had pulled out his driver's license and was showing it to my brother; issued by the state of Illinois. He told us that he had been living in Chicago for the past twenty years and previously worked as a Roadmaster for the Illinois Central Gulf Railroad until they sold off all of their assets in 1988. Most recently he had been an automotive mechanic before arthritis forced him to retire early. S-t-e-p-h-e-n M-c-N-e-a-l was written on his driver's license. The face matched but the name did not. My Father's name was Steven

McNeil. At least that was the name that was printed on my birth certificate. That was the first red flag that caused the hairs on the back of my neck to stand at attention. When I tried to question him about it my mother came to his rescue and tried to explain to me that there were different ways to spell McNeil. Of course there were different ways to spell our last name. Just like there are different ways to spell lots of last names. The difference is, most people don't go around changing the way they spell their last name unless they have something to hide. At least not on legal documents and even if that were true it still didn't explain the different spelling of his first name. I let it go and decided not to dwell on this revelation but I definitely filed the information in the back of my mind in case I needed it for later.

He continued on, telling us stories about where he had been and what he had been doing since he had left us but he still hadn't answered the primary question that had been burning in my soul for the past twenty nine years. WHY? Why had he left us all those years and never come back? If only he had reached out and tried to find us he would have.

What he told us next almost blew me away. He told me that big mama had made him leave. She had run him off and told him to never come back. But that didn't make any sense. The reason that I didn't have my family growing up was because of big mama? I didn't understand. How could she do that to her own daughter or to her grandchildren? All this time I had been harboring resentment towards the wrong person? I had hated my father all these years when it should have been big mama that I was angry with? Lies and secrets can tear families apart and that's why I hate lies.

My mother corroborated my father's story and told me that they decided to move back to the east coast after my grandfather died. They came back to be closer to big mama. They moved in next door to big mama into the rental house that she owned to help take care of her. My brother had been born out in California and by the time they came back to NC mama was pregnant with me. Mama got a job at Rex Hospital while daddy looked for a job during the day. I heard what both of them had said but again something just didn't set right. I couldn't believe that big mama would do this to us so I had no choice but to confront big mama about it.

"Oh, so is that the lie that they told you", big mama asked me as she pushed her chair back away from the table? "They came from California to take care of ME? It was more like they came back home for me to take care of THEM." Big mama was pacing back and forth across the kitchen floor. That could only mean one thing; big mama was mad as hell. "Your mama was not even working when she was in California. She was pregnant with your brother when they got married and moved out to California. He wouldn't let her work. He said he was going to take care of his family and he wanted her to stay at home until after she had the baby. Then after your brother was born he decided that the baby needed her more than she needed to work. You know you were born right after your brother's second birthday. When I think about all that money I spent sending your mama to school and passing her nursing exams for what? So she could sit at home having babies?

Steven was doing a fine job of taking care of his family alright; using my money to do it. I sent for them to come back home so I could stop paying rent. There was no need for me to collect payments from my rental property just to send the money out to California to pay somebody else."

"Well, what about them coming back to help you after grand-daddy died", I asked big mama?

"You call that help? Hell, I didn't need them or their help then. I needed help when your granddaddy was sick. Not after he was dead. Once they moved here your daddy would get a job and just as quick as he would get one he would lose it. His problem was he was always going in somewhere trying to tell people how to run their business and he had a temper too so he would either quit or get fired because he couldn't get along with anyone. People pay you to do a job not for your ideas, unless they specifically ask you. I got him the last job he had from Mr. Black as a favor to me. All he had to do was go to work, mind his own business and help Mr. Black fix cars.

"Fix cars? What do you mean help fix cars?"

"He fixed cars. He was a mechanic's apprentice."

"Wait, I'm confused. He was a mechanic's apprentice? I thought he had a college degree."

"A college degree," big mama laughed. "Child, where on earth did you get the idea that he had a college degree?"

"Mama told me one time when I was a little girl about the day they first met. He had already graduated and was hanging out on campus the day they first met"

"Well that was a lie too," big mama said. He never graduated because he was never enrolled in college. In fact, he had no business on that college campus. He still had babies milk on his clothes."

"What do you mean he had babies milk on his clothes?"

"It's an old saying meaning he was married. He was married with a young child and newborn at home."

"You mean I have another brother or sister or BOTH out there in the world and no one ever told me?"

"Why did you run him off."

"Run him off? Who told you that? I did not run your father away. I wasn't even here the night he left."

"They told me that you ran him away. That you made him leave. Somebody is lying to me."

"Somebody has been lying to you alright but it's not me".

I was so confused but looking at big mama and seeing how furious she was I knew she wasn't lying. I had also seen my mother transform before my very eyes into a different woman ever since my father had arrived and I definitely didn't believe he was telling the full truth. The man had lied about his name for God's sake.

When I got home I confronted the two of them, armed with the recent information I had learned from big mama. Of course they both pleaded innocence and backed each other's story claiming to be victims of big mama. They both swore to me that they were telling me the truth and big mama was the one who was lying.

Just when I thought I had heard it all came the "piece de re-sistance". My father told me that he tried to make peace with his other two children just as he was trying to make peace with my brother and me. So he did have two other children. He acknowledged that his children didn't like him. He said that his oldest daughter had thrown him out of her house when he signed for her mother's body to be released from the coroner when she died.

I don't know why I have always loved to investigate things. I guess it's just something inherent within my nature. It's like once I get something in my spirit I can't rest until I get to the bottom of it. It just keeps nagging and nagging at me until I get it resolved. That's what happened with my father. Something in my spirit kept telling me that things just didn't add up about his story.

That's when I put two and two together and reasoned that if he had to sign papers for this woman's body to be released after all those years than they were still married when she died. He had been married to two women at the same time and suddenly it all made sense why the different spelling of his name.

So his real name was Stephen McNeal. All these years my brother had grown up as Steven Edward McNeil, Jr. His name; our name, was a lie. I couldn't believe that my mother knew all of this and never told us the real truth. What I found even harder to believe was why she would want to ever be with him again. He was a fraud and as far as I was concerned I wish she never would have found him again.

It's ironic that everything I learned about my Father turned out to be a lie; including his real name. In the end, I wished my mother had left my father underneath the rock she had found him under. I guess I had been living in a fairy tale thinking that my life would end happily ever after. My father had shattered my world 30 years ago and now I feel like my world is falling apart all over again. That's why it is so hard for me to forgive Larry right now because I know what it feels like to be deceived. Some stones should be left unturned because you might not like what you find underneath…

CHAPTER 22

Naomi

Dreams Do Come True

There was a heavy silence in the room when Susan finished speaking. Naomi hesitated to lay another heavy story on her friends but what choice did she have. She needed to confront her past in order to move forward and the only way to do that was to pick up from where she had left off in their last session too…

Mr. Davis had been true to his word and given me a key to the diner at the end of my shift. I was still paid up at the motel for two more days but I needed somewhere to store my belongings. I could live in the diner but I couldn't leave my things there without someone finding out what was going on.

I found a small storage unit to store my things in before I went to work that day. I couldn't very well walk around every day with my belongings in tow. That would be a telltale sign that I was homeless. I transferred everything that I would need for the next few days into my backpack. The storage space was not on my normal path so I would need to come back and swap out my clothes every few days or so. Luckily our uniform was black pants and a black top so no one would notice if I was wearing the same pants for a couple of day. Our aprons kept our clothes pretty clean and I could always use a damp cloth to wipe away any stains I got on my pants.

I was so nervous the first night I stayed in the diner. If I got caught living there it would jeopardize everything that I had worked for and then where would I be? I hadn't been in NY that long but I'd already come too far to turn back now. I had no choice. I couldn't turn back. I had nowhere else to go. I had to make this work. I just had to be careful and make sure to cover my tracks.

Each morning I woke up I had to ensure that everything in the diner was left exactly in its place as it was the night before. I didn't dare eat any of the food in the diner. That would be a surefire way to start arousing suspicion; missing food. I made sure to eat in the diner only while I was working my shifts.

The hardest part was the three hour break that I had in between shifts whenever I worked a double shift. Now that I was living in the diner I could actually afford to check into a better motel on my days off which luckily were during the middle of the week and not the weekends. That was my time to shower and wash my hair. I always felt like I had to wash off a week's worth of dirt and grime. On those days, I stayed in the shower until my skin was wrinkled like a prune. On the second night I lingered in the shower just as long as if the extra time would somehow supply my skin with enough soap and water to create a barrier of protection for the week to come.

I started paying for the next week in advance before I checked out the previous week. Even though this motel was better, it was still a motel so I developed a routine. Every Tuesday when I got off from the day shift I would check into the motel and take the sheets off the bed. I would take the sheets and towels with me to the laundromat to wash my clothes for the week. At least that way I knew for certain that the sheets were clean because I washed them myself.

I actually started looking forward to my time at the motel because it became my respite. I could let my guard down and get two full night's rest. I eventually spoke with the maid staff and told them not to worry about cleaning my room whenever I was there. I had become somewhat of a regular. I loved being able to sleep in for two days out of the week.

Because I had nowhere else to go during the time in between my shifts at work or whenever I got bored sitting in the motel room I would hang out at the public libraries. I chose different libraries and different locations within the libraries so I wouldn't stand out as a permanent fixture. My homelessness was actually working towards my advantage because I started using this time and the free resources at the library to start preparing for my GED course that was starting in a few weeks. My first semester for the fall was already paid for and if things continued as planned I would have enough money to pay for the final semester of the program in the spring. Then hopefully by the spring I would be able to find another apartment, or at least a room in a boarding house or something. I wasn't quite ready to entertain the thought of finding a roommate.

I was still living in the diner when school started a few months later. I started marking off each day that passed like an inmate marking off the time of a prison sentence on a calendar. I was so afraid that I was going to get caught that I was almost afraid to breathe but things seemed to be settling down into a routine.

Once I got my GED and enrolled in college it was my plan to use grants, scholarship money and loans to fund school so that I could cut back on my hours at the diner. Eventually I would be able to save up enough money again and I would be able to find a new place to live and stop living in the diner.

My day started at five in the morning. I had everything prepped by the time Slim arrived each morning and he had even taught me how to make the biscuits. There were some nights when I was so tired but I had to keep going. I knew that it would be so worth it in the end.

My GED instructor asked me to stay after class one evening. I couldn't imagine what she wanted to discuss with me but I couldn't take any more bad news. To my surprise she wanted to discuss the results of the first few tests we had taken. I had made perfect scores on all three tests. She wanted me to take the GED practice exam to see how I scored.

I scored ninety-three percent on the exam when she showed me my score the next week. I knew that I had scored pretty high on the placement exam and I'd never had any problems in school but I hadn't expected to score that high on an actual practice exam after only a few weeks of class. She told me that she wanted to give me another random test and if I scored well on that one I might be able to test out of the GED program which meant I might be able to apply to college next semester.

I was so ecstatic about the possibility of starting college earlier than I expected that I slept like a log that night. The first time I let my guard down and that proved to be a huge mistake. I wasn't sure how long I had been asleep but the light in the diner startled me. Maybe it was slim. I looked up at the clock on the wall. It was one twenty in the morning; too early for slim.

My heart sank. Were we being robbed? Instinctively I covered my mouth with both of my hands and took a deep breath; terrified not to make a sound. I closed my eyes as if not seeing them might somehow make me invisible. All I could think about was being back down in the subway with a gun barrel staring me in the face. This couldn't be happening to me again. I had nowhere else to hide so I decided to stay put for the time being praying they wouldn't discover my hiding place.

I guess fear can heighten our senses because I recognized a familiar scent. It was Mr. Davis's cologne. We weren't being robbed but now I almost wished we were. I didn't know what was worse;

being discovered by would be robbers or being discovered by Mr. Davis. Either way I was screwed.

My leg was starting to cramp from being in the same position for the past two hours. I couldn't believe that Mr. Davis was still here. He had made a pot of coffee and I had no idea when he was planning on leaving. I only had a couple of hours before the diner was supposed to open and I was still no closer to getting out of the diner than I had been two hours ago.

About an hour later the break I had been waiting for came when Mr. Davis went to the bathroom. All of that coffee had finally taken a toll on him. This was the chance I had been waiting for to leave the diner. I was just about to walk out the front door when his voice stopped me dead in my tracks.

"I was wondering when you were going to come out."

I felt like an animal that had been stalked and trapped in a cage by a very patient hunter. I had nowhere to hide so I loosened my grip on the door handle and reluctantly turned around to face my captor. As I walked towards him I thought to myself that this must surely be what it must feel like to walk down prison's death row to face your final life sentence. He gestured for me to take a seat in the booth he had been sitting in.

"Ho-o-w long have you known I was in here", I managed to ask? Afraid to look him in the face, I stared at my hands instead.

"I heard you breathing when I stepped inside the diner. You must have been sleeping really hard because you didn't stir until I turned on the lights but I had already been inside for a good five minutes by then."

I scrambled, searching my brain to think of some clever excuse that I could make up to explain why I had been asleep in the diner but I didn't have the energy to lie. For once in my life words escaped me.

"Naomi, I don't know why you were sleeping here in the diner but if you are honest with me and tell me everything I may be in a position to help you."

I looked up at Mr. Davis. I tried to speak but the words still wouldn't come out.

"I can't help you if you won't talk to me."

He handed me a napkin out of the dispenser sitting on the table.

"I'm not crying to gain your sympathy Mr. Davis. I promise. I'm just so, so tired of running and I have nowhere to go. I don't even know where to begin," I explained.

"I've always found that sometimes the best place to start is at the beginning."

What he said was so simple yet somehow it sounded so profound coming from him. So I did as Mr. Davis advised and started from the beginning. He made another pot of coffee and I sat in the booth across from him and told him everything.

Mr. Davis took another napkin out of the dispenser but this time he started writing something on the napkin. "Naomi, I want you to come to this address when you get off work tonight," he said as he folded the napkin in half and handed it to me. "I better get ready to go, Slim will be here soon and it will time you for the two of you to open up the diner."

Mr. Davis packed up the papers he had been working on and stuffed them in his briefcase. He poured himself the last of the coffee in a to-go cup and said goodbye before he walked out the door. I locked the back door after he left and got ready before Slim arrived to work.

When I finished working my second shift I caught a cab to the address Mr. Davis had given me. After paying the cab driver, I walked inside the high rise building and informed the security guard who I was as I had been instructed to do. The security guard escorted me inside an elevator and used a special key that was attached to a clip on his belt to access the penthouse floor.

The elevator doors opened into a private foyer leading to two double doors that were recessed into an alcove entryway. I couldn't believe my eyes when I walked into Mr. Davis's luxurious, Manhattan, penthouse condo. I could see most of the city skyline beyond the stretch of windows as I walked into the main living area. The view was breathtaking.

The guest bedroom suite was just as impressive. A king size, sleigh bed with a leather headboard almost seemed lost in the massive room. I had to pinch myself to be sure that all of this was real. I never thought in a million years that I would have the opportunity to experience such luxury.

After Mr. Davis finished giving me the grand tour of the guest suite he instructed me to open the top drawer of the bureau to retrieve a pair of pajamas.

"I know what you must be thinking but those belong to my daughter."

He had read my mind when I discovered that the drawer was full of clothes.

"She's about your size", he added.

I doubted that these clothes belonged to his daughter because most of the clothes in the drawer still had tags on them. In fact I wondered how many other young girls Mr. Davis had rescued. Something told me that I definitely wasn't the first. I knew that nothing in life was free and nobody was giving away anything without expecting something in return. I didn't know what kind of payback Mr. Davis expected but I had nowhere else to go and no one else to turn to. All I knew was that life had dealt me a lousy hand and maybe, just maybe it was time for the tables to turn in my favor. For now, I was going to take one day at a time until his true intentions were revealed to me.

Mr. Davis bid me goodnight and left me alone to get acquainted with my new surroundings. The first thing I wanted to do was get out of my dirty work clothes and bathe. I hadn't taken a real bath since I had left home. Bathing in the motel bathtub was out of the question. Even in the brownstone apartment there had only been a shower in the communal bathroom. The bathtub had been replaced with an oversized shower. I guess we take the simple things for granted until we don't have them at all.

I soaked in the tub for over an hour; adding hot water to keep the water warm. I scrubbed my body from head to toe and even washed my hair. After I slipped into the silk pajamas I climbed into the center of the bed and slid beneath the covers. I spread my arms and legs back and forth as if I were making angels in the snow. I closed my eyes and reveled in the luxuriousness of the bed; if only for one night, I felt and slept like a queen.

The next morning I looked around the massive closet and found an assortment of clothing to choose from. I felt like I had been given carte blanche on a shopping spree. After a few minutes of perusing through the garments I settled on a pair of jeans and a "bedazzled" tank top shirt. As I suspected the jeans were a custom fit as if they had been designed exclusively for me.

Not sure where Mr. Davis was, I followed the scent of coffee towards the dining room. I found Mr. Davis at the dining room table with his head buried in a newspaper. The dining room was also flanked with wall to wall windows lending itself to another fantastic view of the city.

"Good Morning", I announced as I entered into the dining room and took a seat in one of the chairs.

"Did you sleep well", he asked without looking up from his newspaper.

"Yes I did Mr. Davis."

"Call me Franklin. After all you are my special guest", he said as he lowered the paper to take a sip of coffee. He finally looked up at me for the first time since I had entered the room before putting his cup back down. "So I see my daughter's close fit you nicely. Please help yourself to whatever you like on the sideboard."

When I hesitated, Franklin graciously pointed to the piece of furniture holding a display of assorted fruits and pastries. Now I too knew what a "sideboard" was.

"Would you like any bacon, eggs, pancakes, waffles or anything like that", he asked? "I can have Dobbins bring you something made to order from the kitchen."

"I'll have bacon, eggs, a waffle and grits".

The man who had been standing near the entryway of the dining room left the room without a word and in a matter of minutes arrived carrying a tray. He placed a plate in front of me with a silver domed covering over it. He removed the cover to reveal a plate of bacon, eggs and grits. On the next plate was a golden brown waffle cooked to perfection. I still couldn't believe all of this was happening. This had to be a dream. I was so afraid someone was going to wake me and I'd find out that none of it had been real.

"Franklin I am supposed to go to work today.

"Don't worry, you won't be going back to work at the diner."

My fork stopped in mid-air as I was about to take my first bite of food. My appetite left me as the blood drained from my face. I wanted to kick myself for letting my guard down and getting drawn in again to believing that everything was going to work out in my favor. I let out a heavy sigh as I lay the fork down to rest on my plate.

Franklin chuckled and put the newspaper down for the first time since I had walked in the room.

"Naomi, you have nothing to worry about. I am a very wealthy man. I have seen the hard work that you put in at both diners. You have a strong work ethic and an even stronger will to survive and I admire that about you. I would like to take care of you, give you a place to live and pay for you to go to school."

I was only sixteen but one thing I already knew about life was that nothing comes for free. Was Franklin expecting me to become his "kept" woman or did he have something else more perverted in mind? I wanted to believe what he was saying but I didn't know him. Sure he had always been nice to me but I was sure that his kindness came with a heavy price. I didn't know if I could trust him.

"Please don't take this the wrong way or think that I am un-grateful but why are you willing to do this for me," I asked?

"I want to help you because I wouldn't be where I am today if someone had not been there to help me. So, it's as simple as that; no strings attached", he smiled.

"I don't know what to say."

"Just say yes and let me help you."

I had used people before in the past to get what I wanted but they had been boys and it had always been on my terms. Franklin was a grown man and he was way out of my league. "Let me think about it", I offered smiling back at Franklin.

I stayed with Franklin for three years. He taught me everything and exposed me to all of the finer things life has to offer. In fact he spoiled me. He treated me like I was his daughter and for the first time in my life I knew what it must feel like to have a father who cared. Franklin was the only man in my life who ever treated me the way that I deserved to be treated. In the end all Franklin really wanted to do was help me. It was all the other jerks that I met along the way that tainted my view towards helping people. Before I knew it, I had morphed back into my old self and I've been that way ever since…

CHAPTER 23

Felicia

A Chance For Something Better

Diffidence *[dif-i-duh ns] - lacking confidence in one's own ability, worth, or fitness; timid; shy.*

Sensing a feeling of heaviness in the room, Melina decided to end the session a few minutes early. Susan and Naomi had used up most of the time that night and there wouldn't be enough time for anyone else to start without running over their meeting time. They closed out the meeting, hugged one another and bid their goodbyes.

Melina turned to Felicia after everyone had left and asked her, "Have you ever thought about going back to school Felicia?"

"I think about it all the time but it would be impossible. Number one, I couldn't hide it from Marcus and number two, we couldn't afford it even if he let me go."

"What if I paid for you to go?"

"What? No, Melina I couldn't let you do that. You've already sacrificed enough."

"I want to do this Felicia," Melina replied. "I don't have any children and Tanisha has a full four year scholarship. The only thing that I have possibly sacrificed has been a small portion of my time every other week. Besides, this is what I love to do so I can hardly call that a sacrifice."

"Well, as wonderful as your offer sounds, I wouldn't be able to go anyway. Marcus has the car all day so I wouldn't be able to go to class nor afford to pay the bus fare to get there."

"Have you ever considered online courses?"

Felicia knew she must have sounded like an idiot when she asked Melina, "I've heard of them but what are they exactly?"

"They are classes that you take online on the computer. That way you don't have to go to a traditional classroom. If you don't have a computer I have an extra one you could use," Melina offered.

Felicia had never realized just how sheltered she had been from the rest of the world. Isolation had made her that way though. Thank goodness she had convinced Marcus to buy a computer for the kids a couple of years ago for school.

"Yes, I have a computer at home", Felicia replied.

"That's great! Many of the online courses are self-study and some are instructor led over the internet so you can still use the computer here at night whenever you need too".

"What would I get a degree in? I don't even know how to register or sign up for classes."

"Don't worry about that, I'll help you figure everything out" Melina replied. "I just need to know if you will agree to take the classes."

"I don't know Melina. It's a lot to think about. I mean hiding it from my husband. What about studying and what if I need books? Where will I keep them and what about the library? I'm sure I'll need to go to the library sometime. When will I have time to write papers?

"Felicia, I'll help you. Of course I won't do your work for you but I will help you with resources any way I can."

"What about my job?"

"You don't have to figure this all out by yourself. Susan, Kandi, Naomi, Tanisha, and I have already agreed to clean the building for you. We are each going to take one night a week and you can use that time to study, write papers, catch up on homework or whatever you need. We've got you covered."

Felicia took a step back, covering her heart with her hand. She didn't know what to say. She couldn't believe that they were willing to do this for her. She had dreamt of going back to school but she had never figured out how it was possible and now she was being given the chance. This was a blessing that she could not pass up.

"YES!" Felicia shouted. "Yes, I'll take the classes! Melina, how can I ever thank you," she asked as she wiped the tears from her eyes.

Melina handed Felicia a tissue and replied, "Just take the classes, do your best, and finish whatever you start. That is all the thanks I need."

Melina also handed Felicia several papers with information about various online degree programs and told her to take a look over them. Felicia had a few weeks to decide before enrollment closed and classes started. She was just about to leave Melina's office when Susan walked in.

"Sorry, I'm late," Susan said, looking in Felicia's direction?

"Late for what," Felicia asked, looking over at Melina to make sure Susan had not been addressing Melina instead. Melina shrugged her shoulders.

"I know this is a bit presumptuous but I knew you would say yes and accept Melina's offer. So, I am here to help you clean. If I am going to take over for you on Monday's then I need to learn everything I can about what you do. I am going to job shadow you so that I make sure I clean exactly the way that you do", Susan explained.

For the second time tonight Felicia was speechless. She didn't know what to say. She was so humbled. "Your generosity is more than I deserve", Felicia replied to Susan, blinking back her tears.

"Girl, don't be silly. We are all friends now and you do deserve it. You are our sister and we should help each other whenever we can. Felicia, when you are in a position to help someone else later on, then all I ask is that you pay it forward and return the favor. So come on let's get started. I'm sure Melina has some work to finish and we have cleaning to do."

With that being said, Susan and Felicia left Melina's office and Felicia began training Susan on Building Cleaning 101.

CHAPTER 24

Kandi

Unknown Strangers

//Hello."

"Yes, may I speak to Kandi, Kandi Johnson?"

"This is Kandi."

"Hi Kandi, th-this is Sienna Johnson. I'm your sister."

Kandi's hands fumble almost making her drop the phone.

"Hello Kandi, are you still there?"

"Yes, I'm still here."

"I know you must be surprised to be hearing from me."

Surprised was an understatement, seeing as to how Kandi had never talked to her sister before in her life. Kandi wasn't in the mood for small talk with someone she didn't know and especially not with someone she didn't care for. There had to be a pretty compelling reason for her sister to suddenly call her out of the blue and Kandi wanted to know exactly what that reason was.

"Why are you calling me?" Kandi asked rudely.

After all the years Kandi had spent imagining what her sister's voice sounded like she wasn't excited to talk to her sister for the very first time like she had thought she would be. In fact it was quite the opposite. Kandi didn't want to talk to her sister at all.

She had only seen her sister once in her lifetime and that was at their grandmother's funeral. That was the last time Kandi had seen her father too. He had been making imaginary farting sounds underneath Sienna's neck like he used to do to Kandi when she was four years old. She would laugh and giggle and then beg him to do it over and over again.

During the time of her grandmother's funeral, her father had been cordial enough towards her but he was still being very aloof. Kandi was sure that the only reason he was even speaking to her was for appearance sake. Kandi remembered staring at her baby sister and resenting her for taking her place in their father's heart. Kandi hated her sister so much back then and even now she could feel those suppressed feelings of resentment she had towards Sienna rising up in her again, just as they had for her father the other day in Melina's office.

"I'm sorry to have to call you like this but I'm afraid that I have some very bad news," Sienna informed Kandi. "Our daddy is dead."

This time it took all the strength Kandi had within her not to drop the phone. She stared blankly into space trying to let her brain process the information she had just received. Sienna didn't ask Kandi if she was still there this time. She didn't say anything. Instead the silence permeated between them like a thick London fog shroud with heaviness.

"Sienna had never taken the time to call me before in her life and now the first opportunity she has to contact me she calls me with the news that my father is dead?" Kandi thought to herself. She hated Sienna with every fiber of her being. "She stole the place in my father's heart that I once dwelled. She robbed me of all the father daughter memories I could have had with my daddy. Now she had the audacity to call me and tell me that my father was dead".

Kandi didn't have anything further to say to Sienna so she hung up the phone in Sienna's face.

As much as she hated to, Kandi knew that she had to call her sister back. She hadn't made up her mind yet if she was going to attend her father's funeral but if she decided to attend she would need to know the details of the funeral arrangements. Kandi had purposely waited a few days to call Sienna back. She needed time to regain her composure and time to gain a different perspective of the situation.

However, that hadn't proved to be the case. Kandi still felt the same way she did a couple of days ago when Siena had called her and delivered the news about their father. Her disposition had not changed so she decided she would keep the conversation brief, to the point, and strictly business.

"Hello, may I speak with Sienna Johnson", Kandi announced curtly.

"This is Sienna".

"This is your…this is Kandi. We hung up the phone the other night before I was able to get the funeral arrangements from you so I was calling to get them now if I may."

Sienna was well aware that Kandi had hung up on her the other night but she didn't say anything. Instead, she simply replied, "Yes, yes of course."

Kandi wrote the arrangements down in her date planner.

Sienna began speaking before Kandi could say thank you, "I hope you can find it in your heart to forgive daddy; it wasn't all his fault. My mother forbade him to have a relationship with you. She wouldn't…"

Kandi hung up the phone on Sienna again; cutting her off in mid-sentence before she could finish what she was saying. She didn't want to hear any excuses for her father's behavior because there were none. He was a grown man and there should be nothing or no one able to stop a man from having a relationship with his child if he really wants one. As far as Kandi was concerned he was responsible for the choices he made not to be a part of her life and he didn't deserve her forgiveness.

CHAPTER 25

Susan

When I First Loved You

Susan didn't know why Vanessa would only agree to meet with Larry if he came alone. As far as Susan was concerned, anything that Vanessa had to say to Larry she could have said in front of her. Larry was going to come back and tell Susan everything anyway. Did Vanessa intend to confess her undying love for Larry and beg him to leave me so that she and Larry can give Julian the life he never had?

They had agreed to meet first, at a neutral location, before Larry would meet Julian but Susan still couldn't understand for the life of her why they had to meet. This was about Julian and

Larry; not Vanessa and Larry. Supposedly this meeting was an opportunity for Vanessa to explain to Larry why she had never told him about Julian. Susan wasn't buying it. She was sure this was some desperate plea on Vanessa's part to garner Larry's sympathy for what she had done. Although, Susan had to admit she was curious too and was interested in what possible reason or reasons Vanessa could have had to be so spiteful as to deny her son the opportunity to have a relationship with his father.

Maybe it was actually Larry who wanted this preliminary meeting. Maybe he already knew all about Julian and wanted to explain to Vanessa why he had abandoned her and their son all those years ago. Was he trying to plead for her forgiveness? Susan was being melodramatic but she still didn't trust that woman. Sometimes playing detective could wreak havoc on Susan's mind. The next two weeks couldn't come fast enough. It was her turn to go first at the next session and she couldn't wait.

Susan wanted her friends to know where she was coming from so she decided to start the session by telling them how she and Larry had first met…

People always have a hard time believing that Larry and I waited until we got married before becoming intimate with one another. We both had too much to lose so we decided to wait. It wasn't because we didn't want to. It was hard as hell. There were so many times that we came so close to going in all the way but one of us would come to our senses and push away. I think that's why we got married the same summer we graduated with our masters degrees.

My cousin introduced Larry and I at a family gathering. We were both in Graduate School at The University of North Carolina Chapel Hill. They were Fraternity brothers. Larry was pursuing his MBA and I was getting my masters in Social Work.

Larry was "swole" as they say in slang these days. He was no Mr. Olympus but he definitely had a well-defined, muscular physique.

Even now he stills take very good care of keeping his body in shape but he does it now for health reasons more than anything else.

I was attracted to Larry from a physical standpoint the moment I laid eyes on him but I know it takes more than a physical attraction to make a relationship work. He was very well-mannered and very smart but there were some things that did not particularly appeal to me when we first met. I'm more low-key and Larry is very outgoing. It takes me a long time to warm up to people and I generally don't trust anyone I first meet. People are naturally drawn to Larry so I think I was on guard to make him prove himself to me first.

In college I had made it a rule not to date guys in Fraternities. Since we had surpassed the undergraduate, college level I figured I could bend the rules a little bit in this case. Besides my cousin had told me how much he admired Larry and he felt that Larry was a brother who had his head on straight. My cousin knew me and he knew that I was not the kind of person who would go for any kind of nonsense. He would never introduce me to just anyone.

From the very beginning of our relationship, Larry treated me like a queen. I knew why the moment I met his mother. I know that a woman can't teach her son everything but Larry's mother did a great job raising him. I later learned that Larry had many great male role models in his life despite not having his father around. He had truly been "raised by the village".

I've always looked back over my life and been so grateful that I gave Larry a chance. He's meeting with Julian's mother tomorrow and as much as I want to know the truth, I'm also terrified. Larry is the love of my life. That's why I'll be so devastated if Julian is Larry's son…

CHAPTER 26

Kandi

The Release

Dissociation [dis-uh-soh-shee-aye-shuh n] - Disruptions in aspects of consciousness with one's, identity, memory, physical actions and/or environment.

❚❚Hi Kandi, is everything ok? You seem a little preoccupied," Melina commented.

"Oh, yeah everything is fine," Kandi replied nonchalantly, folding her arms across her chest.

"Are you sure? You know we have no secrets here. Why don't you tell us how you're really feeling? We can see that something is bothering you," Melina observed…

Well, I received a rather unexpected phone call the other day; from my sister. Even though she is my sister and we share the same last name, I didn't recognize the voice on the other end of the line. She was like a stranger to me. Hell, she is a stranger to me. We've never stayed up for late night talks. We've never shared our most intimate secrets. We've never been able to enjoy any of these things that most sisters experience because HER mother had never allowed us to have a relationship.

The irony is, through all that my mother had endured she never turned bitter. In fact she always encouraged me to believe in myself but I guess like every little girl I wanted to be my daddy's little girl and I had been for 8 years. I guess that's why it hurt so much when my daddy left me. I worshiped the ground he walked on. My mother had often told me that I was a daddy's girl from the moment I was born.

My mother always gave me my bath, dressed me for bed and tucked me under the covers. My daddy always read me my bedtime stories, turned out the lamp beside my bed and kissed me on the forehead before saying good night. My father always made me feel safe and secure. He was my hero.

Then one day my whole world was shattered. I will always remember that day so vividly for the rest of my life. They walked into my room; my father first and then my mother. They stood on opposite sides of my bed waiting for the other one to sit down first. My mother stood there with her chin tilted upward and her back straight as a board in a defiant stance. She glared at my father until he finally relented and sat down first. I saw a subtle smirk of victory on my mother's face as she sat down beside me. Her eyes softened when she looked over at me. Her eyes were filled with a sadness that I had seen once before when she told me that our dog snuggles had died. Neither of them said anything. They kept looking back and forth at each other as if they were unsure that they were doing the right thing.

"Kandi, your mom and I are getting a divorce," my father finally said. Now it was my turn to look back and forth at them. They were kidding right I was waiting for them to both start laughing and tell me this was a big joke only neither one of them was laughing. My mom wrapped her arms around me and held me tight, rocking me back and forth like a little baby. She asked me if I understood and I shook my head and said yes to affirm that I understood what they had said all the while a voice was screaming inside my head, "NO", that I didn't understand.

Yes, I understood what they had said. Yes, I knew what divorce meant. I had plenty of friends at school whose parents were divorced but what I didn't understand was why. Why were they getting a divorce and why was this happening to me?

They still loved each other right? Of course they did, so why was this happening. I never saw them arguing. Daddy never raised his hand to hit my mother. They never shouted obscenities to one another. In fact, I had often heard people say what a lovely couple they were. Even my mom's own two sisters used to always tell her how lucky she was to have a husband like my father. She would always chuckle and wave at them dismissively as if they were being silly when they told her how they wished they could have a marriage like hers. I guess that's why they say "be careful what you pray for" because my father had gotten another woman pregnant and that was the reason my parents were getting a divorce.

My mother is one of the kindest, sweetest, most humble people I have ever known. My mother doesn't have a mean bone in her body. I'm not saying she can't be provoked but she is not mean spirited; that's the difference with her. My mother is the calm; the voice of reason; the one who always sees the good in a bad situation. She always searches for the silver lining. I tell people that my mom is the type of person who sees the glass as neither half empty nor half full. She sees the glass as all full; it's just filled to different levels. I wish I shared her optimism but I guess my view of the world became tainted the day my father walked out of my life.

Oh, now don't get me wrong, he supported me financially. He wasn't a deadbeat dad in that respect. In fact, his child support came on time every month like a government check but that's all I had left of my father. His name signed on the bottom of check made payable to my mother with my name scribbled in on the memo section of the check. I knew because when I became a teenager she took me down to the bank and opened a joint account in my name and hers. She transferred all of the child support my father had ever paid her, down to the penny, over to that account and from that day forward I started depositing the checks myself.

Every time I looked at one of those checks, I would wonder if he ever thought about me when he scribbled my name down on the check. K-a-n-d-i, or had writing those checks out for so long become so rote that I was no longer even an afterthought. My mother never needed nor wanted his money that was for sure and neither did I. The checks have long stopped coming but I have never spent a dime of his money. The only thing I ever did with that money was cash it out and opened up a Roth IRA.

I don't even know where my sister got my number from but I guess in today's digital world that we live in it's quite easy to find that sort of information. I just wish there had been another way that she could have notified me. As soon as I heard her voice I knew that it couldn't be good news. I think I was more shocked to hear her voice than I was at the fact that my father was gone. In fact, it really doesn't matter much to me that he just died recently because as far as I am concerned by father has been dead to me for the past twenty-three years.

Now I can FINALLY stop worrying if he'll ever come back into my life because he's dead and he can never hurt me again. In fact, I'm glad he's gone. Good riddance because for as long as I can remember he's caused me nothing but pain. Now I no longer have to wish he was dead because he IS DEAD!...

CHAPTER 27

Tanisha

Inner Turmoil

Anxiety *[ang-zahy-i-tee] - Distress or uneasiness of*
mind caused by fear of danger or misfortune.

❚❚Stop it! Stop it! Kandi, you don't mean that!" Tanisha threw her
hands up in the air yelling at Kandi. "Do you know what I would
do right now just to have my father back?"

Tanisha hadn't meant to startle everyone but Kandi was ranting
and raving out of anger over her father. Kandi's father had hurt
her badly but it wasn't right to be happy over someone's death.

Even when someone dies who has been suffering in pain from an illness or disease you may feel grateful that they don't have to suffer any longer, but who feels happy when someone dies? No matter how much anyone tries to justify it; two wrongs don't make a right.

"I'm sorry Tanisha," Kandi replied as she walked over to comfort her. Kandi wrapped her arms around Tanisha and said, "I didn't mean to make you cry baby."

Tanisha pulled away from Kandi's embrace and turned around to face her.

"I have wished so many times that my daddy were still alive? All of my life I've tried to imagine what it would be like to still have him here with me. I never even got a chance to know him."

"Tanisha, I am so…"

Tanisha cut Kandi off before she could finish her sentence.

"My daddy will never walk me down the aisle on my wedding day. I've never danced with my father and it's my all fault. My father was killed on his way to pick up my birthday cake. Do you have any idea how that makes me feel?"

Tanisha was crying now and she couldn't believe that all of this was coming up from inside of her. All of her pinned up, suppressed pain and hurt was finally coming out. She had never shared these feelings with anyone else before and now her emotions were bubbling up out of control. Kandi tried once more to comfort Tanisha and put her arms around her but Tanisha pushed her away again. Everything was all coming out in the open now and Tanisha had to finish it.

"Do you know how many times I have asked myself what if? What if he had gone to pick up the cake just a few minutes earlier or a few minutes later? What would my life have been like if my daddy were still here?"

"Honey we can't control life or death", Kandi replied. "When God calls someone home we have no control over that. You have to know that whether or not we understand it God has his reasons for everything that he does. You can second guess this your entire life but we can't go back and change what happened."

"Tanisha, I never knew you felt this way," Melina chimed in. "Have you been blaming yourself for your father's accident all these years?"

Unable to speak, Tanisha nodded her head up and down. It was true. Tanisha had been blaming herself all these years for her father's death.

"Look at me," Melina said, cupping Tanisha's face between her hands. "You have to know that this is not your fault. It was your birthday baby and one of the most important ones because it was your first birthday. Your parents loved you. We all did and we wanted your first birthday to be special. The party wasn't even really about you because you didn't even know what we were celebrating. It was for us and there is no way that we would have missed giving you a first birthday party. It's what most parents do. It's a part of most American life; to celebrate your child's first birthday."

Melina held Tanisha in her arms, massaging her back in a circular motion, coaxing Tanisha to give in to her emotions and let her tears flow. Melina kept shushing Tanisha, as a parent would soothe a child, and wiping the tears from her face. Kandi came up behind them. She was crying too as she wrapped her arms around Tanisha and Melina. Before long the other women had joined them and they all stood there in a big circle embracing and comforting one another.

It had never been in Tanisha's plans to discuss her issues in one of the group sessions but now that she had started she felt compelled to continue. It's true what they say that confession is good for the soul.

"I know it sounds crazy to miss someone you never really knew but I do. I miss my dad so much sometimes. I never got a chance to know him but that's what I miss. I regret all of the missed opportunities we'll never have and I regret that I will never get to know him. My dad died when I was one years old. He was on his way back from the bakery picking up my cake for my first birthday when a car came out of nowhere and smashed into the driver's side of his car. He was struck by a drunk driver who ran a red light. I know deep down inside that it's not my fault but somehow I just can't stop blaming myself no matter how hard I try."

"Tanisha, I had no idea you felt that way all these years," Melina admitted.

"I always had trust issues. I've never confided in anyone about my father. Not even my best friend Jordan. Do you know what it feels like to never have that one person in your life who you can feel free to confide everything too; to bear your soul too about your deepest secrets? Well I never had that."

"You've always had friends and Jordan has been your best friend since middle school."

"I know Aunt Melina but I never let Jordan or anyone for that matter get that close to me."

"Why, Tanisha?" Melina asked.

"Because, I didn't want them to die and leave me! That's why. I never let anyone get that close to me because it hurts too much to love someone and lose them."

"Tanisha, I feel so stupid. How could I have been so blind and not have seen or known what you were going through? This is my job and now I feel like I wasn't there for you; like I let you down."

"Aunt Melina, you couldn't have known because I didn't let my feelings show and you WERE there for me more than you know. You shared your stories about my father every time I asked, no matter how many times I asked. I know it was painful for you too but you always told me about him no matter what. I was able to know what my father was like through you."

"You always seemed so happy after I would tell you about him. I had no idea you felt that way."

"I was happy, at the time. It was afterwards, when I was all alone thinking about him that the guilt and regret would set in. There has been many a night when I would cry myself to sleep thinking about him; missing him."

"When your mom remarried you had a wonderful step-father who stepped in and loved you like his own daughter. I just always thought you were so happy."

"Don't get me wrong Auntie I was happy; I am happy. I love my daddy to death. He has stepped in and been a better father to me than most. It's more than I could have ever hoped for. That's why I love him so much and I appreciate him for it. I would not be the young woman I am today without him. He is my father in every sense of the word. There is just that part of me that will always wonder what my life would have been like if my biological father had lived."

"I'm sorry Tanisha," said Kandi. "I hurt so, bad all these years from my father walking out of my life that the only way I knew how to deal with it was to kill him in my heart. I guess I'm so angry with him right now for leaving me and I never got to say goodbye. I don't think I can go to my father's funeral alone. I need you; all of you to be there with me. I can't do it alone."

Kandi started crying and this time Tanisha walked over to her and wrapped her arms around Kandi to comfort her. Melina walked over and embraced them, followed by Naomi, Felicia and Susan. At that moment Tanisha realized that they had become a family in their own special way…

CHAPTER 28

Melina

Forgiveness

*II*I believe that this is the first time in a very long time that I don't know what to say," Melina confessed to the group. "I am supposed to be here helping each one of you and I have missed something that has been staring me in the face for years. I couldn't even see the pain that my own niece was silently suffering through.

One huge lesson in this for me is that sometimes we, as adults, have NO idea what children may be suffering through at times. It's very easy for us to think that children are too young to be affected by certain situations or because they don't speak up or act out everything is fine in their lives.

Children can hold on to a lot of feelings going on inside and internalize their emotions just as we adults can. They can carry guilt and blame themselves for things that are not their fault whether we perceive it or not. But regardless of whether or not what they are thinking is true or not, it is the way that they feel. We can't assume that what is obvious to us will be obvious to them; because that is not always the case.

That's what burns me up about adults who know they are doing wrong to children. Particularly those women who let their hang-ups and insecurities about the men in their lives affect children's relationships with their fathers. A man's relationship with his children should never be a threat to another woman. Most of the time it's not even about the children, it's about the mother of the children. We put so much pressure on the man and threaten him if he has a relationship with his kids. These children didn't ask to be here and every child has a right to know their parents and have a relationship with them. Then these children grow up to be adults and they are still hurting and we wonder why the world is in such the mess it's in."

No one had anticipated this turn of events but it somehow brought them closer together. Crying and comforting one another had proved to be very therapeutic and as a result it had left a solemn atmosphere in the room. It showed that they were all vulnerable; including Melina.

"I asked each of you in the last session to write a letter to your father and to bring those letters to the meeting tonight," Melina reminded them. "Please pull those letters out if you will," she instructed them.

As the women were gathering their respective letters Melina walked over to her desk and grabbed a small stack of envelopes.

"The reason I asked each of you to bring these letters tonight is because I wanted us to perform a symbolic representation of forgiveness. I want each of you to take a moment and silently read your letter once again. When you are done I want you to place your letter inside the envelope and seal it closed."

As the women were rereading their letters Melina grabbed a large ceramic bowl and placed it on the coffee table in the middle of the seating area.

"We are going to address forgiveness. However, before we can even begin to forgive someone we have to know what forgiveness is and also what it is not. The Bible teaches us to forgive others but it never says that we have to keep trusting people who break our trust nor do we have to keep a relationship with people who hurt us but we do have to forgive them. It's ok to forgive and walk away.

When we forgive someone that does not mean that we are tolerating what they did nor are we saying that what they did is ok. In the same respect, forgiving someone doesn't necessarily mean that you will reconcile with them either.

I think that one of the most important things we have to remember about forgiveness is that forgiveness is a process. In most circumstances it will take some time to work through your emotional problems before you can truly forgive. Forgiveness may also be a reoccurring process. You may find yourself having to forgive people or situations multiple times throughout your life.

You need to give yourself permission to forgive and you need to learn how to forgive yourself. Sometimes you have to forgive people even when they have not acknowledged any wrongdoing or asked for forgiveness. This forgiveness is not about them; it's about you. Forgiveness is about letting go of bitterness so that you can begin to heal; forgiveness is for you. Even though I did not write a letter, I have discovered today that I need to ask my niece to forgive me."

Melina walked over to Tanisha and reached out grabbing both of her hands. Melina looked into her niece's eyes and said, "Tanisha I forgive myself for not realizing that you were hurt much more deeply than I could have imagined by your father's death. Can you forgive me and can you promise me that no matter what happens in your life, you will trust me enough to come to me for anything? I can't predict when I will leave this earth but can you open your heart and let me in? In order to fully live you have to be willing to open your heart to love."

"Yes, Auntie," Tanisha cried as she fell into Melina's arms. "I will," she muttered softly between sobs.

After consoling Tanisha, Melina instructed them to place their letters in the envelopes and seal them up. "Now, I want each of you to bring your letter and place it in the ceramic bowl. I want you to forgive the person you have each written your letters too and then burn the letter in the bowl." Everyone was crying by the time the last letter was burned.

"I think today has been a lesson for us all," Melina said, dabbing the tears from her eyes. Her voice was slightly raspy as she replied, "Let us hold hands and conclude this session in prayer." They grabbed hands as Melina prayed for them. They hugged each other one last time and then they all left in silence.

CHAPTER 29

Larry

When The Chickens Come Home To Roost

Larry would be lying to himself if he didn't admit that it blew his mind to learn that he had another son after all these years. A small part of him didn't want it to be true for fear of what it would do to Susan, Devin and Danielle. But he knew. He knew that Julian was his son the moment Julian told him who he was on the phone. What Larry didn't understand was why it had taken so long for him to find out the truth. But he was meeting with Vanessa today and she was going to answer all of his questions.

Vanessa and Larry were meeting at the Blue Coffee Café in downtown Durham. He hadn't thought of her in years but she hadn't changed very much from the way that he remembered her. She was ordering a cup of coffee when Larry arrived at the table. Her voice cracked when she said hello and the awkwardness of the moment keenly became palpable.

"How have you been Vanessa," Larry inquired?

"I've been good and you?"

"I've been great Vanessa. You still look the same after all these years.

She blushed before replying, "Thank you Larry for coming here today. This is very difficult for me."

"Well you must know that I have a million questions."

Vanessa smiled at the waitress when she returned to the table with her coffee. Larry politely declined anything to drink, staring at Vanessa; waiting for her to begin.

She stared into her cup of coffee with her fingers interlaced together and took a dep breath. "Larry, Julian is your son. I know I should have told you a long time ago."

"Wait," Larry said, holding up his hand to stop her from saying anything further. His eyes narrowed as he racked his brain trying to figure things out. "I'm confused. When did you find out you were pregnant?"

"I knew that day that I told you," she whispered.

"You mean you knew way back then? You looked me in my face and lied to me?" Larry closed his eyes and covered his mouth with his clenched fist. He shook his head back and forth in disbelief. "How do I know you are not lying to me now?" Larry asked Vanessa poignantly.

"I'm not lying to you Larry. Not this time," Vanessa said, unable to look Larry in the eyes. "The only reason I lied back then was because when I first told you that I was pregnant you weren't happy about the news of my pregnancy."

"But I came back and told you that I would be there for you, that I wouldn't abandon you," Larry replied, tapping the table with his index finger as he spoke each word.

"Yea, you did but your first reaction was how you truly felt. I would have become a burden to you. Having a child would have kept you from "living your dream". Weren't those your exact words?"

"Yes," Larry admitted. "But I was just thinking out loud, before I had a chance to really think about what I was saying. I was caught totally off guard and I just reacted. Everything was already in place for me to leave and attend Grad school, but even still, if I had known that you weren't kidding, I would have stayed. I could never walk out on my child. I could never leave them. I have an obligation to take care of my children as a father."

"EXACTLY! You would have stayed out of obligation and I wanted you to stay out of love."

"I would have grown to love you Vanessa. I'm sorry. I didn't mean it that way, it was just too soon. I meant that I would have naturally grown to love you if we had only been able to spend more time together because I was already falling for you," Larry said, as he reached out and touched Vanessa's hand.

"I was falling for you too. I felt guilty, like I had trapped you somehow and forced you to give up on your dream. You would have grown to resent me and I couldn't live with that."

"No, I wouldn't have resented you Vanessa and I wouldn't have had to give up my dream. What you didn't know was that I had also gotten accepted into the MBA program at Texas Southern University as well. I chose UNC because I would be closer to my family. Once I got over the initial shock of you being pregnant I came up with an alternate plan. I could have stayed with my company and reduced my work schedule down to thirty hours per week. I would have still been eligible for benefits and still been able to continue with school."

"I didn't know," Vanessa sighed.

"When I came to tell you about my new plans and how it could all work out you told me you weren't pregnant. Remember? You told me that you just wanted to see what my reaction would be; I was so confused by that. Honestly, it threw me for a loop. I was disappointed that you would play games with me like that about having a baby. You caused me to question my own judgement of character. I couldn't understand anyone doing something like that. So, when I left for school I decided it would be best to just cut off all ties with you."

"I thought I was doing you a favor."

"Doing ME a favor?" Larry raised his voice. "How could you think you were doing me a favor by keeping me from knowing my son?"

"I-I, don't know. I made a mistake; a terrible mistake that I will have to pay for, for the rest of my life," Vanessa replied through her tears. Larry snatched his hand back as Vanessa tried to reach out to touch his hand to apologize.

Larry felt as if someone had just sucker punched him in the gut. He was too angry and shocked to feel anything at the moment. Vanessa kept crying and repeating over and over again how sorry she was for what she had done. Despite Larry's anger nothing could change what had already been done. Larry hated to see anyone hurting and no matter his feelings at the moment he was convicted by her tears and handed her a tissue in an effort to comfort her.

"I would have stayed Vanessa. I would have stayed."

Vanessa looked up at Larry staring into his eyes and cried even more. She knew that Larry was telling the truth. Words went unspoken between them but they were both reflecting in their own way and they both realized how differently their lives would have turned out if Larry had truly known back then that Vanessa was really pregnant.

"When can I meet him?" Larry asked Vanessa.

"He's very excited to meet you."

"I'm excited to meet him too."

"I was hoping that you would feel that way so he came along with me. In fact, he drove me here because I was too nervous to drive. He's outside waiting in the car. I can call him and tell to come in if you're sure."

"Yes, I'm sure Vanessa. Please tell my son to come in so I can meet him."

The moment Larry laid eyes on Julian there was no denying that Julian was his son. It was like seeing a younger version of himself as if he had been transported back in time through some magical time portal. Larry could see three generations of Thorpe men standing before him. Julian was tall and slender with a chiseled chin. He had the signature thick and bushy eyebrows that almost all the Thorpe men had, along with a widow's peak hairline. As the saying goes, he was the spitting image of Larry. In fact, Larry couldn't see any resemblance of Vanessa in Julian, although he was sure there were some if he searched long enough but right now all he could see was his twin. If the truth be told, Julian looked more like Larry than Devin did.

Larry's throat constricted as he thought about all of the opportunities he had missed out on to watch his son grow up. He had done nothing wrong but he was consumed with guilt. He stretched out his arms to embrace his son as tears flowed heavily down his face. Even though Larry couldn't make up for twenty two years of lost time he held on to his son as if he could. Julian returned the embrace, hugging his father with all his might; afraid to let go. Larry knew that people were watching their exchange but that didn't matter. The only thing that mattered was holding on to his son and letting him know how much he loved him.

Larry felt mesmerized looking at his son after all these years. Seeing Julian for the first time, Larry loved him just as much as he had loved Devin the first time he laid eyes on him after he had been born. It didn't matter how old Julian was. The initial feeling of seeing your child for the first time is still the same.

Julian sat down at the table next to his mother as Larry explained, "Julian, I'm not trying to make excuses or evoke your sympathy, but I didn't know I had a son. I didn't know about you."

"I know, my mom told me everything. She told me what she did but I know my mother and I can understand why she did what she felt she had to do. It's not about blaming anyone. None of that is important to me. All I care about is getting to know you, if you will let me, and moving forward from here," Julian replied.

After meeting Julian in person, Larry knew that it would take some time to be able to forgive Vanessa but he was so proud of Julian. His words spoke volumes of the kind of young man he was and despite what she had done, Larry knew that Vanessa had raised their son well.

Susan was waiting in the kitchen for Larry when he got home. She was flipping through the pages of a magazine trying to find something to do to preoccupy her mind. She was anxious to know what happened but the news would break her heart.

"It's true isn't it," Susan asked Larry before he could say anything.

"Yes, Susan. Julian is my son. It's true."

Susan's shoulders slumped down in defeat as if the very life had been sucked out of her. Her face was awash with despair and Larry felt an invisible wall go up between them. He had never meant to hurt his wife.

"You had a son all those years and you NEVER said a word?"

"I didn't know. As God is my witness I didn't know. I love you Susan and you know I love my children, but no matter how much I love you I won't let anyone stand in the way of trying to establish a relationship with Julian. You know that I would have been there for him if I had known about him. You wouldn't respect me if I walked away from him now and I wouldn't respect myself."

"You're right," Susan said. "I don't expect you to walk away."

"So how is this going to affect you and me?"

"I don't know Larry. I just don't know," Susan replied as she got up from the table and walked away.

CHAPTER 30

Felicia

A Ray of Light

Felicia had been racking her brain for the past couple of days trying to figure out how she was going to ask Marcus to let her attend Kandi's father's funeral. She thought about sneaking behind his back and going, but she decided against that idea. The consequences would be too great if she got caught. Instead, she opted to be upfront and just ask him if she could go. If he said no, then she would contemplate another alternative.

Recently Felicia had noticed a few subtle changes in Marcus. It was as if he were being nicer to her lately which had made her hopeful that he might say yes. He had never been this nice to her in their entire marriage. She first noticed it a couple of weeks ago. He started putting his clothes in the hamper before he got into the shower. He really surprised her when he carried his dishes over to the sink last week and rinsed them off. She didn't know what had sparked this change in Marcus but it had given her the courage to ask him about attending the funeral. She just prayed that this change in him would last.

She knew that Marcus would ask a ton of questions before he would ever agree to let her go. But she couldn't tell him the complete truth. She had to lie and pretend that Kandi was a co-worker of hers so she spent most of the day rehearsing and fabricating details of the funeral. She had to be prepared and ready with an answer for anything he might ask her.

She also scrubbed the house from top to bottom and slow cooked a Yankee pot roast with all the trimmings; one of Marcus's favorite meals. A clean house and good meal might increase her chances of convincing Marcus to let her go. At least it couldn't hurt.

Marcus called her later that afternoon to tell her that he was going to be late. Felicia hated the days when Marcus worked overtime. It usually meant that he would be in a bad mood when he got home. Now, depending on how late he was, she might not even have enough time to talk to him about the funeral before she had to go to work. She decided to remain positive and prayed that he would make it home in time for them to talk.

Marcus pulled into the driveway around six o'clock. Felicia only had thirty minutes to spare before she needed to leave for work. Marcus was whistling when he came through the door so that was a good sign.

"Mhmm, is that pot roast I smell?" he asked.

"Yes. Why don't you go ahead and take your shower and I'll make your plate. The kids and I have already eaten."

This was one of the rare times that Felicia and the kids ate without Marcus; whenever he worked overtime.

"Looks like you did some serious house cleaning today. You cooked one of my favorite meals. What's going on?"

"Nothing," Felicia shrugged.

"I know you better than that Felicia", Marcus eyed her suspiciously. "What is it?"

"Well, I wanted to ask your permission to attend a funeral."

"A funeral? Who died?"

"A woman from work; I mean her father died."

"I thought I told you not to get all chummy with anybody at work."

"I didn't, we just work together and she broke down at work the other night. I felt kind of sorry for her because she said she hadn't seen her father in about twenty five years; that part was the truth. She helped Mr. Jamison with my shift when I was out of work a while back."

Marcus flinched when Felicia mentioned the incident that happened several months earlier.

"So I just want to be there for her during her time of need", Felicia smiled, hoping that Marcus would not dwell on the reminder of the incident and become agitated.

"How will you get to the funeral?" he asked.

"I could take you to work or I could ride the bus."

"When is the funeral?"

"Friday."

Marcus hesitated, "I'll tell you what. You can take me to work and then use the car to drop the kids off at school. Then I guess you could go to the funeral."

Felicia suppressed her enthusiasm before replying modestly, "Thank you Marcus".

"Wait." Felicia's heart skipped a beat. She was afraid that Marcus had changed his mind. "You know what, when you and the kids pick me up after work on Friday, how about we go out to eat at a real restaurant? How does that sound?"

"That sounds good Marcus", Felicia replied. "Really good."

She couldn't remember the last time they had been out to eat at a real restaurant. Marcus felt that Felicia was home all day so she had plenty of time to have a hot meal on the table every day. Whenever they did eat out on the weekend ninety-nine percent of the time it was always fast food. An establishment with a drive through was not Felicia's idea of a restaurant.

"Have a good evening at work Felicia and tell your co-worker I'm sorry for her loss."

"I will Marcus. I'll see you when I get home tonight."

She kissed him on the cheek and he smiled up at her before she left to go to work. Yes, Marcus was definitely changing.

CHAPTER 31

Kandi

A Day of Reckoning

Rationalization *[rash-uh-nl-i-zay-shuh n] - To ascribe one's acts or opinions to causes that superficially seem reasonable and valid.*

Kandi stood in front of the mirror staring at her reflection. It had been a long time since she had really looked at herself. Of course she "looked" at herself in the mirror on a daily basis but she rarely looked past the reflection in the mirror. Today was different. Her eyes were almond shaped with full, thick eyelashes that rarely needed mascara. She took the lipstick out of her purse and traced the shape of her lips with the lipstick before pursing her lips together to blend the color evenly. Today there was no denying it. She had her father's nose and her father's lips. She even had the trademark Johnson dimples. They had been passed down from her grandmother, to her father, and then to her.

Sienna had called Kandi back after being hung up on for the second time and left a voicemail message, "I've wanted to call you so many times and just talk but I could never think of the right words to say. I was afraid that you might hate me. Sometimes when daddy and I were all alone he would talk about you. I know you may not believe this but he really did love you. I hope you can find it in your heart to forgive him one day. Well, I guess I'll see you at the funeral. Bye."

Kandi had hated her sister for a very long time and part of Kandi wanted to continue hating her now. However, as much as Kandi may have wanted to continue hating Sienna, to feel better, she knew that Sienna was as much a victim as she was. It wasn't Sienna's fault. None of this was her fault and she did not deserve to suffer for it any longer.

Kandi finished combing her hair before she turned out the light and left the bathroom. She sat on the bed contemplating whether or not she should still go to her father's funeral. But, even as she sat on the bed, not moving, she knew that she was going because it was the right thing to do and she always did what was right.

She had not seen her father in over 21 years. She couldn't believe that he was actually being buried in Raleigh and not back in Phoenix, AZ. Kandi thought how ironic it was that his wife had finally allowed him to make a decision for once in his life. Too bad it happened during his death and not while he was alive.

Sienna had extended an invitation for Kandi to meet them over at the hotel and ride to the church in the family limousine. But Kandi couldn't imagine subjecting herself to the awkwardness of being confined in a car with Sienna and her mother so she declined the offer. She needed her own private time alone with her father to say goodbye and the only chance she would have to do that was before the service started; before everyone else arrived.

Trent pulled into the parking lot of the church as Kandi was overwhelmed with memories. This had been her grandmother's church. Kandi remembered coming to Sunday school whenever she spent the night with her grandmother and she would bring Kandi to vacation bible school every summer before she passed away.

Kandi loved her grandmother and she knew that her grandmother had loved her. Deep down inside Kandi's grandmother had always tried to make up for her son's absence from Kandi's life. She tried to reason with him to have a relationship with Kandi. Whenever Kandi would visit her grandmother she would always call Kandi's dad. Kandi would hear her grandmother trying to convince him to talk to her on the phone but he never did. Instead, her grandmother would just smile at her when she got off the phone and hug her with all of the love she had inside of her as if she could fill the void in Kandi's heart that her father had left there. Kandi could never forget the deep remorse that she remembered seeing in her grandmother's eyes.

Trent opened the door to the sanctuary and interlaced his arm with Kandi's arm. Her knees felt like they were beginning to buckle and she couldn't bring herself to walk down the aisle just yet. She motioned for Trent to stop and take a seat on the back pew. She could feel her pulse beginning to race and a knot was forming in the pit of her stomach. Her hands became clammy and her face felt flush. This was silly. What did she have to be nervous about? She had every right to be here yet somehow she still felt like a stranger at her own father's funeral.

She finally regained her composure and worked up the nerve to move from the pew they were on and started walking towards the front of the sanctuary. She paused momentarily in the middle of the aisle and tightened her grip on Trent's arm. He covered her hand with his and reminded her that he was there for her to lean on; everything was going to be alright he reassured her.

Kandi held on to Trent's arm in a death grip as they continued down the aisle until they were standing just a few inches from the front row pews of the church. Every ounce of anger and resentment vanished the moment that she saw her father lying there in his casket. The strong, self-motivated, determined, confident woman that she had become melted away as if she had been morphed back to the eight year old little girl that she was when her mother and father had told her they were getting a divorce. She felt like the air was being cut off from her lungs and she was certain that she was about to hyperventilate.

She stood there frozen; unable to move. She was overwhelmed with grief and it took an insurmountable amount of strength to fight back the tears. She couldn't do it. The floodgates were opened and all the penned up pain that she had held on to for so many years came rushing out.

Kandi let go of Trent's arm and walked closer to her father's body. Her vision was blurred as she could barely see past the cloud of tears that had formed in her eyes. She examined her father's face intently as she had examined her own just an hour earlier. He wasn't smiling but she saw the creases in his face that marked his undeniable dimples. Of course his hair was greyer than she remembered and his face was fuller and more mature but there was no denying he was her father. All the resolve she had was gone as she looked down at her father lying there. She missed her daddy so much and no matter how angry she had been with him all these years, she realized that she still loved him. The tears were rolling involuntarily down her face. Her makeup was ruined but she didn't care. It didn't matter to her. Nothing mattered to Kandi anymore except being able to see her father again, even if it was for the last time.

A few minutes later Trent came up and whispered in her ear, "Baby, the family has arrived."

Kandi glanced back over her shoulder and saw the limousine parked outside in front of the church. She didn't want Sienna or her mother seeing her like this. She refused to give them the satisfaction of seeing how badly she was hurting so she made a beeline to the restroom before they got out of the limousine.

Kandi reapplied her makeup to repair the streaks in her foundation that had been caused by the tears streaming down her face. It had been a wise decision not to wear mascara so she wouldn't look like a raccoon with black smudges underneath her eyes. However, there was nothing she could really do to reduce the redness or puffiness so Kandi decided to wear her shades for the time being.

Trent was waiting for her when she came out of the bathroom. He reached out and held her hand in his. He kissed her on the cheek and reassured her again that everything was going to be alright. Kandi didn't know what she would have done if Trent were not there by her side. He was her rock.

They came around the side of the church so that they could line up with the family. Coming face to face with her sister for the first time as an adult was the hardest thing Kandi could remember having to do in a very long time. Her stomach felt like it was flipping cartwheels as they walked closer towards the gathering of people lining up in front of the church. It was more a feeling of dread than anything else.

She could feel people watching her. She knew that most of them were watching to see how she was going to react. She didn't even know how she was going to react but she wasn't going to make a spectacle so if anyone had come to her father's funeral today to see a show they were going to be highly disappointed. She was just glad that she had her shades to cover her eyes. It provided her an imaginary shield of protection to hide behind.

Kandi saw a young woman at the front of the line who appeared to be in her mid-twenties. She was standing next to a woman wearing a black hat tilted to the side so that it was partially hiding her face. The woman was holding a handkerchief and Kandi could see her periodically dabbing the corners of her eyes. She assumed that the two women were Sienna and her mother. Sienna was a beautiful young woman. They had the same complexion and dimples too. She looked like their father; she looked like Kandi. Seeing Sienna in person changed Kandi. Kandi resolved in her spirit that Sienna was her sister and they shared a bond. Despite everything they were family.

Sienna smiled and gave a small wave to Kandi. Kandi didn't respond but kept her head held high with grace and dignity as she walked passed them to take her place in line for the funeral procession. Her feelings towards her sister were softening but she wasn't exactly ready to welcome her into her life with open arms just yet. It was going to take time but today was not about mending her relationship with her sister; it was about burying her father.

Kandi was talking with her friends after the service and introducing them to Trent when Sienna's mother came over to speak to her. "Hi Kandi. I'm Diane Johnson, William's wife. Your stepmother", she announced and extended her hand towards Kandi.

"I know who you are", Kandi replied, not even bothering to turn her head in Diane's direction to acknowledge her presence. Instead, Kandi kept talking with her friends, as if Diane wasn't even standing there. Visibly scorned, Diane pulled her hand back when Kandi did not reciprocate her handshake."

"I just wanted to come over and apologize to you in person."

"Don't you think it's a little too late for that now?" Kandi hissed. "I'm a grown woman. I don't need your apology."

"Well, I-I, just wanted you to know that everything wasn't William's fault. Most of it was mine and I'm so sorry that I didn't allow your father to contact you all these years. I felt insecure."

Kandi turned around this time to face her step-mother. "You felt insecure? WHY? You had the man. I was HIS daughter! Why would you feel threatened by me? You denied me a relationship with my father AND my sister! Your apology is not going to bring my father back. It's not going to give me back the years I missed or the relationship I could have had with him."

"I know. I know that now. If I could undo the wrong I've done I swear to you I would", Diane pleaded.

"Well you can't now, can you?"

"If there is anything I can do all you have to do is ask. I'll do anything you ask me to do."

Kandi had not meant to make a spectacle but before she realized what she had done she had slapped Diane. Kandi knew that her mother had taught her to act like a lady at all times but Kandi was tired of always doing the right thing. She wasn't trying to seek revenge but sometimes people get what they deserve.

"Oh, you'll do anything I ask? Anything? Can you bring my father back from the dead? Huh, can you do that?"

"No, I can't," she whispered, covering her cheek with her hand. She lowered her gaze to the ground unable to look Kandi in the eye.

"You know what, it's amazing to me how people do wrong all their lives and then when they are on their death bed or someone dies they become remorseful and want to do what's right. You slept with my father, knowing he was a married man and got pregnant. Then you tried to elevate your illegitimate daughter above me and now you want to say you're sorry? Well you can take your apology and you know what you can do with it because it's too late now to say you are sorry," Kandi let the words seethe from her lips before turning and walking away from Diane.

They had just discussed forgiveness in their last therapy session but Kandi just wasn't ready yet. She was willing to forgive Sienna but she couldn't say the same for her step-mother. Kandi and Sienna had both been victims and she had already missed too many years away from her father. She didn't want to waste another fifteen or twenty years not having a relationship with her sister. Forgiveness is a process and maybe with time she could learn to forgive Diane but for now she was only concerned about her sister.

One Year Later

CHAPTER 32

Felicia

A Brand New Day

It had been a long, hard year hiding the truth from Marcus but Felicia had managed to do just that. In less than two weeks she would graduate and receive her certificate in web design. Marcus had really changed over the past few months and for the first time they were beginning to get along like a real couple with a real marriage. She really wanted to invite all of her family and friends to her graduation to celebrate her achievement but she couldn't. She had been tempted once to tell Marcus everything

196 | SHERRY J. MCFARLAND

but she wasn't sure that his newfound kindness had evolved quite that far yet.

So instead Felicia had arranged for her certificate to be mailed to Melina's office and she would have to sneak it into the house somehow. There was only one final exam that stood in her way which she would be taking in four days. Working towards her certificate was more than she ever expected. It had done wonders to boost her self-esteem and she felt like a new person.

She finally felt like she could do anything that she set her mind too. Even though the women in the group had never looked down their noses at her or given her any reason to feel inferior around them, earning her certificate made her feel more of an equal with them. She could finally hold her head up high. Felicia knew that her children would be proud of her just as she was always proud of them and someday she would be able to tell them all about it. She wanted them to go to college even more now because she knew how empowering college could be.

Being around Melina, Naomi, Susan, Kandi and Tanisha had helped her in more ways than they would ever know. As self-fulfilling as obtaining her certificate was, she wanted and needed more. She wanted to make a difference in people's lives. She needed to pay it forward so she found a job as a freelancer designing web pages. Working as a freelancer would allow her to put her web design skills to use so that her certificate wouldn't go to waste.

Kandi helped her create an LLC for her freelance business and Melina let her use her office address for filing the paperwork. Tanisha's father prepared all of Felicia's tax documentation so that she could be paid through the LLC tax identification number. Felicia couldn't use any of the money without Marcus finding out but she planned to leave the money in the LLC account and use it one day for her children's education. Hopefully by then she would be able to tell Marcus and he would be grateful instead of angry that there was enough money saved up to send them to college.

Felicia could smell bacon cooking and thought she must be dreaming so she rolled over and kept sleeping, but the smell was getting stronger. She opened her eyes and noticed that Marcus's side of the bed was empty. She was wide awake now and that was definitely bacon she smelled. But who was in her kitchen cooking bacon. She stepped into her slippers beside the bed and grabbed her robe hanging on the back of the bathroom door.

She peeked in on the kids but they weren't in their rooms. She didn't think she had slept that long but maybe she had. She looked in the living room expecting to find them watching cartoons but they weren't in there either. There was only one place left to look and that was the kitchen. Marcus was in the kitchen all alone.

"Where are the kids?" Felicia asked Marcus.

"Oh no, you got up too early. I was going to surprise you and bring you breakfast in bed."

This had to be a dream. Marcus didn't cook. Not even when she was sick. He would order take-out; and now breakfast in bed. Felicia was shocked beyond belief. She didn't even know he knew how to cook.

"To answer your earlier question, my sister picked up the kids earlier and we have the whole day to ourselves," he said, handing her a cup of coffee with sugar and cream just the way she liked it.

Felicia wrapped her hands around the warm mug and closed her eyes as she took a sip of coffee. Marcus pulled out a chair and motioned for her to sit down. She was speechless but she had to know what was going on.

"Marcus what is all this for? Don't get me wrong, I love it but I'm just confused. What's the occasion?"

"You work hard to take care of me, the kids, and this house. I know I haven't shown you the appreciation you deserve. I'm trying to change Felicia, I really am because you deserve better. So I called my sister to pick up the kids so that I can spend the whole day pampering my wife."

Felicia couldn't believe all of this was happening. It almost seemed too good to be true. For the first time in her marriage she was actually beginning to feel happy. This was the husband and marriage she had always wanted.

198 | SHERRY J. MCFARLAND

CHAPTER 33

Kandi

The Smell of Success

Obsessive *[uh b-ses-iv] - Abnormally dominate or preoccupy the thoughts, feelings, desires or actions of a person.*

Kandi could feel something brewing in the air. The office had
been a buzz all week. It was that feeling you get when everyone
is in on a secret but you. People divert their eyes when you catch
them staring at you or all of a sudden the conversation changes
gear when you enter a room.

Kandi had been right. All of her suspicions were confirmed when
she entered the executive briefing room for the bi-weekly staff

meeting. Everyone yelled "Surprise" as soon as she walked through the door. The banner that was hanging across the picturesque window read "Congratulations Kandi Johnson, Junior Partner."

Mr. Weinstein was holding a new wall plaque with her name "Kandi Johnson" and the title "Junior Partner" printed directly beneath her name. She was astatic that her plans and dreams had finally come to fruition. She had made Junior Partner. All of her sacrifices and hard work had finally paid off. She couldn't wait to tell her family and friends.

It was somewhat bittersweet that her dad would never know; it had been almost six months since her dad had passed away. But at least she would be able to share the good news with her sister Sienna. Kandi had called Sienna about a month after their father's funeral. Things had started out a little slow in the beginning but that was understandable. They had a lot to catch up on. Their relationship was growing and evolving but they at the point where they talked about every other week now. They had both decided not to talk about their father and dwell on the past but to move forward and build a relationship as grown women and as sisters.

Trent was the first person Kandi called but he didn't answer his phone so she called her mother and told her the wonderful news. After all the speeches, congratulations, and well wishes from everyone she set out on the task to move her things from her old office to her new executive office. Each of the executive offices had an oversized mahogany desk with a matching hutch and credenza directly behind the desk. In the corner near the window was a small table with four chairs. She would definitely have to buy a few more things to fill up the empty spaces and make the office feel more like hers but she couldn't be happier with her new office.

She tried calling Trent again a couple of hours later and still there was no answer from his phone. Oddly though, now the calls were going straight to voicemail. If she didn't know better she would have sworn that he had turned his phone off. She decided to call Davenport's to see if she could get a last minute reservation. Generally that place was packed but she was hoping that she would get lucky with it being a week night.

"Maybe Trent already knew about the promotion and was out secretly setting things up for a celebration," she thought to herself. That wouldn't surprise her because that was the kind of man Trent was. He was very thoughtful and resourceful and that was another of the many qualities she loved about him. She dialed Trent's number thirty minutes later and for the second time her phone call went straight to his voicemail. She hung up this time without leaving a message.

Kandi's mother insisted on taking her out to lunch to celebrate the good news. Kandi felt a little guilty because she had turned her mom down the last two times her mom invited her to lunch because she had been working on cases. Her mom was not hearing any excuses today. Kandi had worked hard for this promotion and she deserved to be celebrated.

"Hi Mommy," Kandi greeted her mother before giving her a kiss. No matter how old she got she would never be too old to kiss her mother or stop calling her "mommy".

"Hi Kandi, I'm glad you could finally find time in your busy schedule to have lunch with me," her mother replied with subtle sarcasm. They both laughed. That was also her mother's way of politely scolding her for turning down her lunch invitation the past two times.

"I know mommy, but I have been SO busy," Kandi replied.

"I know sweetie, I'm just teasing you and making you feel guilty at the same time," Ms. Johnson smiled.

"It's working because I do feel guilty and I miss our lunch dates. I really do."

"Well, at least all your hard work has paid off. I'm so proud of you Kandi."

"Thank you," Kandi replied blushing.

"Now maybe you can finally settle down and get married and make me some grandbabies. You have devoted enough time to your career. You are going to let life pass you right on by and then you will be left with a life of sorrow and regrets. Family is too important Kandi."

"Mom please, not you too. I can't take you nagging at me to get married. I still have more plans for my career and I get enough badgering from Trent."

"Well he's right you know. Speaking of Trent, I know he must be so proud of you too?"

"He doesn't know yet, or at least I haven't told him. I haven't been able to reach him on the phone. His phone keeps going straight to voicemail."

"You don't think anything is wrong do you?"

"No, he would have called me by now, unless he can't call me."

"Well, don't worry," Ms. Johnson said dismissing the notion that anything was wrong. "I'm sure that everything is just fine. He'll call you as soon as he can."

Initially Kandi wasn't worried until her mother told her not to worry. This was not like Trent at all. Even if something were wrong with his phone he would have found another way to call her by now; especially if he already knew about her promotion. There had to be a logical explanation so she decided not to worry and focused instead on enjoying a long overdue lunch with her mother.

CHAPTER 34

Naomi

Dust Yourself Off and Try Again

Compulsion *[kuh m-puhl-shuh n]- An uncontrollable impulse to perform an act, often repetitively, as an unconscious mechanism to avoid unnacceptable ideas and desires which can raise anxiety.*

Naomi was so confused about Lance and it was driving her crazy. She had never had a man turn down her advances before and God knows she had tried everything she could think of to seduce him. They had been dating for over a year now and he refused to take the bait. She felt so out of control with Lance and that scared her. She was falling for him hard. She was smitten by his charm and charisma. Not to mention that he was handsome, wealthy and very kind towards her.

She was pretty sure that he felt the same way about her, otherwise she wouldn't have wasted this much time trying to develop a relationship with Lance. But maybe she had been going about this all wrong. Maybe it was time to try something different. After all, it has been said that the definition of insanity is doing the same thing over and over again while expecting different results. For the first time, in a very long time Naomi sincerely wanted a different result. She wanted to develop a serious and committed relationship with a single man and she wanted that relationship to be with Lance.

Despite the many negative experiences Naomi had with men over the course of her life, her entire view of all men was not completely tainted. She knew plenty of good, wholesome, honest and decent men. Take for instance Kandi. She had a good man and she was about to let him slip through her fingers. Naomi didn't want that to happen to her and Lance.

Life had dealt her a lousy hand and now maybe the cards were turning in her favor. Perhaps the women's group was having a positive influence on her. Who knows, maybe even God himself was finally blessing her with good fortune. She didn't know what was going on but she was grateful and she didn't want to do anything to mess things up.

If she was going to turn over a new leaf and try something different, she needed to start with her wardrobe. She needed to tone down the sexy a couple of notches, yet still remain sophisticated and stylish, so she called Kandi. They agreed to meet for a girl's day of shopping in a couple of weeks and Kandi would serve as Naomi's fashion consultant. She had to laugh at the thought of going to someone else for fashion advice but Kandi had that Michelle Obama style about herself and she would be able to help Naomi find more conservative clothing than what she usually shopped for.

Tonight Naomi finally decided to slow things down a bit and let Lance see the "real" Naomi. No fancy restaurants or fancy clothing; just a simple homemade dinner with no strings attached. Tonight was all about simplicity and being vulnerable.

She rented two movies for them to watch after dinner. One action flick for Lance and one romance flick for her. She wanted to show Lance different facets of herself and she also wanted to see how he would adapt to watching something that she enjoyed. She wasn't trying to put Lance through any kind of test but they needed to spend time around each other doing normal, day to day things. Naomi wanted to make sure that they were compatible beyond the physical attraction that she definitely had for him.

Little did she know that was exactly what Lance was looking for but he wasn't going to force her into it. It had to happen naturally and it had to be on her terms. It was long overdue for him to get to know her beyond the surface level but that couldn't happen until Naomi was ready. She had been very vague and elusive every time he asked her about her past or her family and if she wanted their relationship to move any further it was time for her to trust him. Family was important to Lance and he had to know that it was important to Naomi too.

"So, beautiful lady, I never hear you talk much about yourself. We've been dating for a while now and I want to know everything there is to know about you," Lance said.

"There's not much to tell," Naomi replied. She had been dreading this day but she knew it was coming. She had to finally tell Lance the truth about her family or lack thereof.

"Naomi, I've been transparent with you since the day we met and I've shared my entire life with you. Why won't you trust me with yours? What about your family? You know all about mine so why don't you tell me about yours? They can't be that bad. No matter what you tell me I won't leave. You can trust me Naomi," Lance replied as he softly brushed Naomi's cheek with his hand.

Naomi closed her eyes as she grabbed Lance's hand squeezing it softly taking a deep breath for strength. "I had a hard life Lance; a very hard life. I didn't have anyone to rely on so I lost trust in people. It's hard for me to admit but I've turned bitter, self-centered and egotistical over the years and I don't like those qualities about myself anymore. I used to view those attributes as a sign of strength and power but I know that's not true anymore. I've observed you over the past year and you have taught me how to be humble. I finally realize that real strength and power lies in humility."

"See, now that wasn't too hard was it? You can trust me with anything. I won't bite. So what about your family? Do you have any siblings?"

"No, I was an only child and I never knew my father."

"What about your mother? Where is she?"

"I honestly don't know. I left home when I was sixteen and I've never looked back; until recently," Naomi replied, unable to meet Lance's gaze. Knowing how close Lance was with his family made Naomi feel embarrassed about the estranged relationship she had with her mother. "When I left home I went to New York and I've been taking care of myself ever since. In the beginning I met a really nice man who helped me get my education but just when I was beginning to gain faith in people I eventually met someone who turned out to be a real slime ball. He almost destroyed my life so when you have no one to depend on but yourself it can turn you into a bitter and cynical person. You learn to keep your guard up and you don't trust anyone but I've met some really amazing people over the past year and the best person of all, is you. You all have made me realize that family is important. So I've actually been thinking about my mother a lot lately. I've been thinking about trying to find her."

"Naomi, I think that is a great idea. If you truly want to change and if you want to find your mother than all you have to do is start."

"I don't even know where to begin."

"Start where you left off. Start with the last place you were together."

"I'm terrified of the thought of trying to find my mother but you make it sound so simple. I don't know if I can face her alone and even more terrifying to me is the thought of never finding her. What if she's no longer living? What will I do then? Lance, I'm not trying to involve you in the middle of my chaos and I know this is a lot to ask of you but do you think you could help me find my mother?"

"Naomi you don't have to worry. I want to be involved in every aspect of your life. I'll be right by your side. You don't have to be afraid of anything. I'll be with you every step of the way, if you want me to."

"Yes Lance, I want you to be there. I need you to be there with me. I need you Lance."

Lance reached down and cupped Naomi's face between his hands and planted the most tender, loving kiss on her lips she had ever had. He gazed deeply into her eyes before kissing her on her forehead. She wrapped her arms around him as he held her in his arms.

Of all the times she had tried to seduce Lance this was what she had really wanted all along. All she ever wanted was for the man she loved to kiss her, to hold her in his arms, and to make her feel loved and protected. She knew without a shadow of a doubt that she loved Lance with all of her heart and soul and she didn't want to conquer him anymore. She wanted him to conquer her. She felt so safe in his arms and it was at that moment that Naomi surrendered her heart to Lance Davenport.

CHAPTER 35

Lance

The Black Knight

Things were finally beginning to shift gears in Lance and Naomi's relationship. She stopped throwing herself on Lance and actually allowed him to take control of their relationship. When she finally decided to let down her guard with Lance, he was able to see a beautiful vulnerability open up within her. She exhibited an uninhibited trust in him. He knew that it had taken a tremendous amount of effort on her part to let him in.

Naomi was a very intriguing woman who Lance perceived had been badly hurt in her past. Naomi was like most women who have been hurt before. They put on a tough façade as a defense mechanism in order to survive. Lance knew that deep down inside Naomi was a pearl that needed to be cultivated to show her true beauty. When Naomi truly and freely gave her heart to a man he will have discovered a rare gem and Lance wanted that man to be him. He wanted to unveil the true treasure that lied deep within Naomi. However, he would never play games or manipulate a woman into loving him.

Lance only knew how to be himself which was a hardworking, respectable, reliable, and loving Christian man. He treated women as queens for the true beings that they were created to be. He respected women and treated them with the respect they deserved as his father had respected his mother and taught him to do. He always treated women with respect even when they didn't demand it for themselves.

He was not trying to cultivate Naomi into being anything she was not. He was simply letting time take its course and whatever was meant to be would be. Lance was a true believer that whatever God has destined will come to be.

He had to give Naomi an A for effort though. She had put up a good game. Naomi was a provocative and desirable woman that any man would find hard to resist. It took all Lance had within him and a whole lot of praying not to follow her when she had invited him inside her apartment after their first date. He hadn't been sure if she was wearing that red dress or that red dress had been wearing her. The dress looked like it had been painted on her skin. It was hard to tell where the dress began and her body ended. Lance had kept his hands in his pockets for a reason and the only relief he got came by way of a cold shower thirty minutes later when he got home. Even thinking about the vision of her now in that red dress was doing something to him and he didn't want to have to take another cold shower.

The black dress she wore on their second date hadn't been much better. It had the same effect on him. Naomi had not been able to hide her disappointment on that date when he rejected her second invitation. The disappointment was written all over her face.

Lance had to admit he was amused at times with Naomi's attempts to seduce him over the past year they had been dating.

Being a former professional athlete and wealthy businessman, Lance had seen almost every trick in the book. The difference with Naomi was: he knew she wasn't a gold digger and she wasn't malicious. She was a manipulator for sure because she was used to being in charge. The difference with Lance was; he couldn't be manipulated.

Lance never sacrificed his standards and he never bowed down to pressure. That's how he was able to sustain his credibility as a successful businessman. Always maintain your dignity and stay true to yourself. Slow and steady wins the race and Naomi had slowly but surely come around and let Lance pursue her.

Naomi had a past but everyone does. People change. Lance was not concerned with a person's past as much as he was concerned with where they currently were and where they were going. Two of his philosophies were "Each new day is an opportunity to be and do better than you did yesterday" and "Learn from the past and move on".

Even though he grew up living a privileged life he never took it for granted or lived his life like somebody owed him something. Instead, he always took full advantage of the life he had been given and never thought that he was better than anyone else. He considered himself to be blessed so he made the decision early in life to never waste his blessing.

Lance felt honored when Naomi finally trusted him enough to tell him the truth about her childhood and her relationship with her mother. After hearing her story he admired her strength and tenacity to survive. Leaving home at sixteen had forced her to feel that she only had herself to depend on. It was a major breakthrough for Naomi to confide in him which meant that their relationship was finally moving to the next level and he couldn't be happier.

CHAPTER 36

Susan

Yours, Mine And Ours

The past year taught Susan a lot about forgiveness; most of which she learned from Melina and Julian. Susan and her father were never able to develop a real relationship and she was ok with that. At least she knew who her father was now, she knew where she came from, and she had the opportunity to meet him so she had no regrets. Maybe her father had done the best he could and maybe he hadn't but she had learned to forgive him and accept him for who he was anyway.

She wished things could have turned out differently but who knows. Maybe in the end, before it was too late, things might change. Her life had turned out well and everything was in a good place again. It still took some getting used to but she had a new son; she had a great husband who was an awesome father, and she had met a group of amazing women who had become lifetime friends.

Susan couldn't help but admire Julian. He was a great respectable young man. Regardless of the circumstances, he was her husband's child and her children's brother, and for those reasons, she considered Julian her son. Melina had taught Susan that we are all a sum of our life experiences and even though people can be faced with the same set of circumstances, everyone doesn't react the same way. She still didn't condone what Vanessa did but she had learned to forgive Vanessa too for the sake of her family and out of respect for Julian.

Her relationship with Larry was stronger than ever. The day he stood up to her and told her that he would not walk away from Julian whether she approved or not was the day she gained all the love and respect back for her husband; especially after her father could not do the same for her. It took time, maturity and wisdom, not to mention the therapy sessions, for Susan to realize that you have to be willing to meet people where they are. She also now realized that she had been carrying around a lot of anger that had made her set some unrealistic expectations of people. She now understood that not everyone can or always will meet your expectations; that was just a fact of life.

They were planning for Julian to come to NC in the summer for a family reunion so that he could meet the rest of his extended family. Devin and Danielle had embraced Julian as their "big brother" the moment they found out about him. Vanessa had never married nor had any other children so Devin and Danielle were Julian's only siblings. They had been keeping in touch with one another through Facebook, phone calls and texting.

It was amazing to Susan how a simple phone call a little over a year ago turned her world upside down and for it all to be right side up again because of Julian Larry Baker; her new son. God

212 | SHERRY J. MCFARLAND

has a way of breaking us down to build us back up. God showed Susan what unconditional love is really all about.

CHAPTER 37

Tanisha

Love, Unconditionaly

Irrationality *[ih-rash-uh-nal-i-tee] - The quality or condition of acting without reason; acting without normal mental clarity or sound judgement.*

"I don't know who's going to be the most sad when
you leave; me, your mom & dad, or Jordan," Melina said as she wrapped her arms around Tanisha.
"I'll only be gone for two years Aunt Melina."

"I know but California is so far away. We've been together since
the day you were born. You couldn't find a graduate program anywhere on the east coast?""Yes, they have some great programs here
on the east coast but I'm ready to spread my wings and Stanford

University has the best program for my area of concentration. At least I didn't go out of state for my undergraduate degree. I stayed right here in good ole North Carolina," Tanisha said in her best imitation of a southern drawl. "Two years will be gone in no time. I mean look at how fast this past year has flown by." "Yea, you are right Tanisha. Two years is not a lot of time before you will be back in good ole North Carolina," Melina laughed. "Unless you meet some nice guy and then you might stay in California forever." "Nah, I could never stay away from the east coast forever." "Never, say never; love can make you do some crazy things." They both laughed. Tanisha was going to miss her talks with her Aunt Melina the most. She had been more than an aunt, she had been a friend. It was going to be a big transformation for her to move to California but she was looking forward to starting the next chapter of her life. She had so much to be grateful for and working with the women had taught her so much about herself. She discovered how blessed she was to have been given a second chance to have another father in her life. Her Aunt Melina had helped her understand that her father's death was not her fault and she had finally learned to stop blaming herself.

Tanisha was young but she knew what it meant to get so caught up in your own guilt, living in the past, wallowing in self-pity, or consumed with un-forgiveness that you forget to live. She didn't have all the answers why God does what he does but she trusted him and thanked him for giving her the best "Daddy" in the world. Her dad had loved her unconditionally from the moment they met even though he wasn't her biological father. She knew that in the end it really didn't matter; the bonds we build are based on relationship and love.

"Hi daddy, can I come in?" Tanisha asked as she entered her dad's office. He was working from home this week in preparation for Tanisha's graduation on the weekend. "Sure honey what's on your mind?" her dad asked. "Nothing. I just wanted to tell you how much I love you and how much you mean to me." "Well I love you too honey but where is all this coming from? You trying to bribe me about something," he chuckled. "No." Tanisha stated biting on her bottom lip. He knew something heavy was weighing on her mind. "I love you so much dad because you stepped in and filled a void in my life where some men wouldn't or couldn't. You loved me unconditionally." "Now you really have me worried. You must want something really big," he chuckled. "Daddy, I'm being serious!" "I know baby, I'm just teasing." "I'll be honest, I used to imagine what my life would have been like if my dad had lived. I know he was a great man but you are too and we need to tell the people we love how much we love them. I know we have always said "I Love You" in our family but sometimes we need to tell the people why we love them. How many times have people said I know they love me but. There shouldn't be any buts. "I did what any real man would have done Tanisha. All I ever prayed for God to do was give me a good wife whom he chose for me and children to love, to protect, and that I could teach about his ways. I didn't specify how he should do it because that was not my job; that was God's job. My job was to praise him and honor my promise by taking care of what he entrusted me with to the best of my ability. I love you Tanisha. I always have and I always will until the day I die." Tanisha always knew her dad loved her but now she knew why.

CHAPTER 38

Trent

The Fork In The Road

Trent was attracted to Kandi the moment she stood up in class and recited her entire 10 year plan; albeit the instructor had only asked for the class's five year plans. He admired her drive and determination. She exuded a sense of confidence about herself that wasn't the least bit cocky or arrogant. In fact, Trent still admired Kandi's tenacity, however, sometimes too much of a good thing can be detrimental. Unfortunately, for where they were in their relationship and where Trent was at this point in his life, Kandi's strong will and determination was negatively affecting their relationship.

The fact that Kandi was beautiful both on the inside as well as the outside was an added blessing. It's rare to find a person whose inner beauty matches their outward beauty as well. What he loved most about Kandi was that she was genuinely a very caring, honest, and giving woman once you really got to know her. Trent knew that Kandi's drive and determination personified OCD behavior but he knew that it wasn't intentional.

Trent was a very patient man but every man has his limits. As much as he tried to understand Kandi's decision to wait to get married he just didn't want to wait any longer. In his opinion six years was more than enough time. He felt that Kandi's real issue was trust and he had done everything within his power to show her how much he loved her and she still didn't trust him.

Sometimes you have to force the other person's hand to see what they will do, and Kandi had shown Trent that she was not ready to get married, so he decided to move on with his life. He didn't want to give up on their relationship but he felt like his back was up against the wall. He had been ready for a long time to settle down with Kandi and build a life together. He finally accepted the fact that what is meant to be will be and he had to start living what he believed. One thing he had learned about life's ups and downs is that "this too shall pass".

Trent looked up from the sofa when he heard Kandi's key in the door. He had taken the day off and had been waiting for her to get home. He knew about the promotion because Mr. Weinstein had called him a couple of days ago to tell him about it. Trent had declined his offer to come to the office for the momentous announcement. Somehow he had felt that it would be a little callous of him to be there knowing what he was about to do.

Kandi's hands were full with a bouquet of flowers, a bottle of champagne, and a dozen balloons. Trent jumped up to assist her because she could barely close the door behind her.

"You should have called me and I could have met you in the garage to help you carry this stuff inside," Trent replied.

"I've been calling you all day and you haven't returned my calls so I didn't KNOW you were home. Where have you been all day?" Kandi asked.

"I had a lot of running around to do today and a lot of last minute things to take care of. What is all this stuff anyway," Trent replied, trying to change the subject.

"Well, if you had answered your phone, you would know by now that I made JUNIOR PARTNER," Kandi shouted with enthusiasm as he followed her into the kitchen and put the flowers on the center island.

"Congratulations baby," he said as he gave her a congratulatory kiss. She was beaming with excitement. Obviously she had moved past the missed phone calls. He decided to test the waters when he asked, "So, does this good news mean that now we can celebrate your promotion along with wedding plans?"

"No, this means that now I only have to wait about two more years to make senior partner, THEN we can celebrate my promotion and wedding plans."

"That was exactly what I was afraid you would say."

"Are you really going to go there today of all days? You know it took me almost four years to make Junior Partner. It will take twice as much hard work to make Senior Partner in half that time. Do you know how much time goes into planning a wedding? I can't do both."

Her words were a sober reminder of what Trent needed to do.

"Kandi, you are the love of my life, the woman that I want to spend the rest of my life with. The woman that I want to be the mother of my children and the woman I want to grow old with. Baby I want ALL of you or none of you.

"You already have all of me."

"No I don't. You have given all of yourself to your career and to the firm. I can't do this anymore."

"What do you mean you can't do this anymore? What are you saying?"

"What I'm saying Kandi is that I'm tired of waiting but I love you enough to let you go."

"Trent I'm sorry you feel this way. I'm sorry that you are not willing to fight for us for just a little while longer."

"I'm sorry too Kandi but I can't continue when I feel like I'm the only one in the fight."

"So this is it? You're just going to walk away from everything that we have been building together? So are you putting me out?"

"I know this was my apartment but you are more than welcome to stay here as long as you need to. I've paid up all the rent on the remainder of the lease. I moved all of my things out already this morning."

"So that's why you weren't returning my phone calls? You were moving your stuff out before you even knew what my decision would be?"

"Kandi, you and I both knew what your decision was going to be. I was just trying to give you one last chance to change your mind and you didn't."

Kandi didn't say anything because she knew he was telling the truth. Trent felt like a part of him was dying inside but she had left him with no choice. He grabbed his suitcase and headed to the door. He laid his keys on the console table in the foyer and turned to look at Kandi one last time. She wouldn't turn around and look at him but he could tell from the way her body trembled that she was crying. He never imagined that it would come to this. The irony of it all was he felt like they were getting a divorce but they had never been married.

CHAPTER 39

Marcus

Should've Known Better

Aggression *[uh-gresh-uh n]- Violating by force the rights of another. Any offensive action, attack or procedure.*

The guys at work were teasing Marcus that he must really love his wife because he always went straight home when their shift was over and he never hung out with them after work. He didn't always show her but he did love Felicia. He knew he was wrong and that's why he had been working so hard lately on being nicer towards her. She had been putting up with his crap for ten years and she didn't deserve it. She had stood by his side when no one else would so it was way past time that he started treating her more like a wife instead of his servant and whipping boy.

He liked the way that their relationship had changed over the few months. His sister had even started watching the kids for them recently while they went out to the movies a few times. Marcus knew Felicia was still afraid of him even though he hadn't put his hands on her in over a year. He hadn't meant to get that angry with her but when he got mad it was like something took over him and he couldn't control his anger; it was like he wasn't himself anymore. He hadn't grown up in an abusive family so he didn't know where it came from. Actually he did. He was angry with the world because he had lost his dream of having a career in football. His life with Felicia was a constant reminder of everything he had lost.

He knew it wasn't her fault but it had been so easy to blame her. He was only 17 years old when it happened. Back then he didn't appreciate the fact that his injury could have been worse. Some players have been paralyzed from the type of injury he had. But instead of being thankful for the small things he had let his anger and bitterness send him into a downward spiral of self-pity and animosity.

Through it all Felicia had been there and was still with him. It was past time for Marcus to treat his wife with the love and respect she deserved so he bought Felicia the pair of shoes she had seen the last time they were in the mall. He knew how much she wanted them and he rarely bought anything for her unless it was her birthday, Mother's day, or Christmas so he decided to surprise her. He got the step ladder to hide the shoes up on the shelf in her closet that was beside his.

When he lifted the sweaters to put the shoe box underneath them he found an envelope addressed to Felicia with a different address than their house. The envelope had her name on it but it was also marked to the attention of a Dr. Melina Bradshaw. At first Marcus thought it might be her receipts from the hospital last year. He took a second look at the envelope because the address seemed very familiar and then he realized the address was the office building that Felicia cleaned. He never knew there were any medical doctors in that building. He reached inside the envelope and pulled out a piece of paper:

Internet and Design Technology Certificate
Specializing in Web Design

Felicia W. Riley

Has Satisfactorily Completed all Requirements
Being Duly Awarded
As Approved by the Board of Trustees and Faculty
Of North Carolina State University
Department of Engineering and Technology

Marcus found Felicia's college certificate. He was confused. He had honestly been trying to change and then she pulled a stunt like this. How could he have been such a fool? "I bet she was so proud of herself that she was sneaking behind my back and who is this Dr. Melina Bradshaw?" Marcus thought. "Where in the hell did Felicia get money to pay for school? When did she take these classes? All this time she had been playing me like I was a chump!"

Marcus sat in the living room, in the dark, for two hours thinking back over the past year. After a while he couldn't sit still anymore. He started pacing the floor feeling like a restless, caged animal. All he could do was think about how many times Felicia had smiled in his face knowing the whole time that she was sneaking behind his back. He kept punching his right fist into the palm of his left hand thinking over and over again how his wife had deceived him.

He saw the headlights from the car shine through the blinds when Felicia pulled into the drive. He sat back down and waited in the dark for her to come through the front door. Felicia came through the door but she didn't realize that Marcus was sitting there watching her until he spoke.

"You must feel pretty good about yourself don't you?"

"Oh my God," Felicia cried out clutching her heart. "You scared me."

"You've been real slick."

"Marcus, what are you talking about and why are you sitting here in the dark?" she asked as she switched on the lamp on the coffee table by the door.

"So when were you going to tell me about school?"

"School? There's nothing going on with the kid's school. Why, did one of their teachers call?"

"Don't play dumb with me! I found your little certificate. I've been nice to you and this is how you repay my kindness? You've been sneaking behind my back taking classes?"

"Wait Marcus let me explain!"

"Explain what? How you've been lying to my face every day for how long?"

Before she had a chance to speak Marcus slapped Felicia across the face knocking her into the wall. She tried to scurry away from him but he grabbed her by her hair. He spun her around and hit her in the face with his fist. She reached up striking his face with her nails. Marcus let go of her hair when he felt the burning sensation on his face and reached up to feel the whelps where she had scratched him.

She tried to get away from him again. This time he grabbed her around her waist and threw her into the wall. She fell to the floor. He reached down to pick her up again and she started swinging back at him. Felicia had never fought Marcus back before which sent him into a fit of rage. He started beating her uncontrollably with his fists.

"Go ahead and kill me. Do it. Do it dammit. At least I'll die knowing that you'll be in jail and my kids will be raised by my mama. So just kill me!" Felicia yelled at Marcus.

Felicia's newfound defiance caused something in Marcus to snap. He wrapped his hands around her neck and started choking her. He kept squeezing tighter and tighter. The more she wiggled and writhed and fought to release his hands from around her neck, the stronger his grip became. It was as if he had lost control

224 | SHERRY J. MCFARLAND

of his faculties. Something was telling him to stop but his hands wouldn't release their grasp from around her neck.

"Stop daddy, don't kill mommy", Megan cried out.

If it hadn't been for their baby girl he probably wouldn't have stopped. He loosened his grip and Felicia's body slumped to the ground. For the first time, Marcus was afraid of his own anger. He realized that he was truly capable of killing his wife. DeMarcus and Jazmine had come out of their rooms too and all three of his children were huddled over Felicia's body crying. He didn't know what to do. Felicia was unresponsive. He didn't know if she was dead or alive so he grabbed his keys and ran out the front door.

CHAPTER 40

Naomi

The Missing Piece

Naomi was second guessing Melina's advice to try and find her mother. But wasn't that what she had come to therapy for--to get advice? She had no idea where her mother was after all these years. She didn't even know if her mother was still living. Suddenly she felt an overwhelming sensation of guilt about the way she had left home all those years ago.

Back then there was a big part of her that just didn't care and she wanted to hurt her mother as much as her mother had hurt her. She honestly really didn't think her mother would even miss her when she was gone. But time and experience had taught Naomi that two wrongs don't make a right. It was time for her to face her demons. She needed to do this in order to move forward with Lance. She didn't want to bring any old baggage into their relationship.

Regardless of how her mother felt towards her she needed to forgive her mother. She needed peace in her life and it felt good to be able to totally trust someone the way she trusted Lance. She realized that there are some good people in the world and not everyone will hurt you. If you keep your heart under lock and key you may never find true love. You have to be willing to get hurt sometimes in order to grow. It's a part of life.

For the first time in a very long time Naomi was putting her complete trust in a man. She had shared everything with Lance so there would be no secrets. She wanted and needed him to share this journey with her. So either way, good, bad or indifferent he would be there with her every step of the way. She had to go back to the beginning where the source of all her pain began. She had to go home.

Naomi felt a quickening in her chest when she got out of the car and looked up at the house she had grown up in. Maybe this was easier said than done. But there was no turning back now. She had come all this way so she had to do this. She walked up the steps and knocked on the door. She turned around and looked at Lance while they waited for the front door to open. He smiled at her reassuringly. She knocked again. Still no answer, but just as they were about to turn around and leave a woman's voice could be heard on the other side of the door.

"Who is it?"

"Hi, my name is Naomi. Naomi Miller. I used to live in this house when I was a little girl and I moved away when I was a teenager.

I-I was actually trying to find my mother; I was hoping she still lived here."

There was a pause of silence before the door swung open. A petite elderly woman opened the door. She examined Naomi from head to toe and then looked past her to get a close look at Lance who was standing behind Naomi.

"How long have you lived here if you don't mind me asking?"

"I've lived here about ten years now," she replied. "I moved here to be closer to my family after my husband died."

"I'm sorry for the loss of your husband," Naomi sympathized.

"Oh, its ok honey, my Henry lived a long full life and now he is resting in peace with no more pain," she smiled at Naomi and Lance.

"Did you ever meet the former owner?" Naomi asked.

"Yes, I met the owner briefly at the closing. She appeared to be a nice lady but there was something about her eyes though that seemed so sad to me; like she was missing something or someone."

"Maybe that was my mother," Naomi said, more as a statement than a question.

"I'm not sure honey. Maybe you can check with one of the neighbors. Do you remember Ms. Gillespie across the street?"

"Yes."

"Well she still lives there. Maybe she knows where your mother moved to. Why don't you go and ask her."

"Ok, thank you! Thank you for all of your help. I'll go ask Ms. Gillespie."

"You're welcome honey and good luck finding your mother," the elderly lady replied before she closed the door.

Naomi and Lance walked across the street to Ms. Gillespie's house. Her flower beds were just as beautiful as Naomi remembered. Ms. Gillespie had given many of the neighbors, including her mother, seedlings from her flower beds but no one's garden ever grew as beautifully or bountifully as hers. Ms. Gillespie's flowers had even been featured in the local newspaper once when Naomi was a little girl.

Ms. Gillespie was sitting on her front porch. She peered over her glasses scrutinizing the two strangers who were walking up her sidewalk. "Naomi? Naomi Miller, is that you?"

"Yes ma'am"

"Lord chile bless my heart, I haven't seen you in years" she said raising her hand towards heaven. "Are you trying to give me a heart attack?"

"No, Ms. Gillespie."

"You know, you still look the same. I'd recognize you anywhere. You haven't changed a bit; still beautiful as ever."

"Thank you," Naomi blushed.

"Well where in the world have you been hiding all these years?"

"I was in New York for about 10 years and then I moved back to Raleigh about 6 years ago."

"SIX years ago! You mean to tell me that you have been living in Raleigh for six years and this is the first time you've been back over here in your old neighborhood?"

"Yes ma'am."

"I seen you over there snooping around at your old house. You ought to be ashamed of yourself running off like that and staying away for so long. I know things won't right between you and your mama but it still won't right the way you just snuck off like that. You had all of us around here worried sick. The po-lice came 'round here asking everybody questions. They was looking for you everywhere. Nobody knew if you had been abducted or just run off, but I knew."

"I'm sorry Ms. Gillespie. I didn't mean to worry anyone I was just trying to get…"

"Get back at your mama. I pray you are not still holding on to a grudge towards your mama. Don't you know chile something like that will eat away at you like a cancer. It ain't good for you. You got to learn how to forgive."

"I know Ms. Gillespie and that's why I'm here. It took me a long time to figure that out and the help of a lot of good people," Naomi replied, smiling at Lance. "I'm trying to find my mama; if I'm not too late. Ms. Gillespie, do you know where my mother is?"

"She moved over off of Sanderford Road. Baby let me go and get her address for you."

Mrs. Gillespie reappeared a few minutes later and handed Naomi a piece of paper with her mother's address written on it.

"Now I haven't talked to her in about a year but I am sure she still lives there."

"Thank you Ms. Gillespie", Naomi replied and gave her a big hug.

Naomi's mother's house was about ten miles from her old neighborhood. As they rode to her mother's house she noticed that not very much had changed over the past sixteen years. She knew the area well because she had passed this way every day on her way to school before she moved away. Now she thought how ironic it was that she had managed to stay away from this side of town for the past six years but stubbornness and anger can make you do that.

She took a deep breath as Lance parked the car on the street in front of the house. There was a car parked in the driveway underneath a carport. She didn't recognize the car but it would stand to reason that her mother would not still be driving the same car she had when Naomi was in high school.

Lance kissed her hand before getting out of the car and coming around to open the passenger side door. She checked her hair in the mirror to make sure it still looked ok. For the third time today Naomi and Lance walked hand in hand as they went to the front door and Naomi rang the doorbell hoping to find her mother.

"I'm coming, let me get my purse," a voice behind the door said. "You're early, I thought you weren't gonna get here for an-other…" her mother gasped in mid-sentence and clutched her chest when she looked up and realized Naomi wasn't the person she had been expecting.

"Hi mama. It's me, Naomi." She reached out and grabbed her mother's arm to keep her from stumbling backwards.

"N-Naomi? Oh my God, Naomi," she cried. Tears were rolling uncontrollably down her face as she reached up and touched Naomi's face. "Is it really you?"

"Yes mama it's really me." Naomi replied, unable to control her own tears.

They reached out and hugged each other as if they were holding on to one another for dear life. Naomi could not remember her mother ever holding on to her like that her entire life. She was comforting Naomi and Naomi was comforting her. They were both forgiving one another without having to say so.

"I love you Naomi. I have prayed for this moment for so long. I didn't know if you were dead or alive. After a while I thought you were never coming back and I would never see you again," she said crying. "Thank you Lord, thank you Lord," she kept repeating over and over again.

"I love you too mama. Can you ever forgive me?"

"Naomi I was not a loving mother and I pushed you away. I don't blame you for leaving. I blame myself. You never deserved to be treated that way and I'm truly sorry can you forgive me?"

"Yes, mama I forgive you."

"Thank you Jesus! My baby is home!"

CHAPTER 41

Kandi

Serendipity

Kandi couldn't believe how stupid she'd been. She was so educated but she had not exercised any common sense when
it came to her relationship with Trent. She had a man that most
women would die for and she let him slip through her fingers.
She was so hung up on her own insecurities that she let it blind
her to what she had standing right in front of her.

She was well aware that Trent was a good man but she took
it for granted that he would wait for her. She had become too
comfortable in their relationship. She let her feelings, her goals,

and her ambitions become more important to her then Trent. Relationships are about compromise and she was too stubborn or too foolish to take Trent's wants and needs seriously.

Kandi knew that Trent didn't take her for the sentimental type but deep down inside she was. Like most little girls it was her dream to have a beautiful wedding. Unbeknownst to Trent, Naomi knew every detail of her wedding even though he had never seen her sitting around perusing through bridal magazines. She had dreamt of having a spring wedding so that they could get married at Duke Gardens in Durham, NC; the place of their Alma Mater and the place where they first met. The reception would be held at the Duke Inn.

She didn't know why she was so surprised by Trent walking away from their relationship because they were so much alike. Kandi knew that what he wanted was just as important as what she wanted. He was a man of conviction so it was only a matter of time before he would concede and move on. Trent would never stand in the way of her true desires no matter how much it hurt him to walk away.

Kandi had to question herself. At the end of the day did it really matter? If you are blessed enough to find a man who loves you unconditionally, who puts your needs over his own, a man who would lay down his life to protect you then you have a rare gift that should be treasured. Wasn't that what really mattered?

It was as if somehow her father's death and reconciling with her sister had finally set her free. She was free to finally love someone with her whole heart again. She didn't have anything to prove to anyone; not even to herself. She had finally come to her senses but she could only pray that it wasn't too late. She never imagined her life without Trent and she didn't know what she would do if she couldn't get him back. She had to make things right again between them. That was the only way.

Trent had agreed to come over so that they could talk and that was a positive sign. At least he was willing to hear Kandi out. She was so nervous when the doorbell rang. It was so strange for Trent not to use his key and let himself in.

"Hi Kandi," he said. She wasn't prepared for the awkwardness that filled the air between them.

"Hi Trent, come in," Kandi said as she held the door open for him to step inside. He looked so good. "Can I get you anything to drink," she asked?

"No I'm fine"

She didn't like how formal he was being with her. His demeanor was making her even more nervous than she already was.

She sat down on the couch facing Trent with her legs folded underneath her. "Thank you Trent for coming to hear what I have to say."

"Of course Kandi I would give you the courtesy of hearing what you have to say but Kandi you already made Junior Partner and you still don't want to get married so I really don't know what else there is to say? We've already hashed through this over and over again. What's changed?"

"I realized that life is too short and I was being stupid by letting you walk out of my life."

"You realized all of this after I walked out? Now all of a sudden you've had a change of heart?"

"No, I made up mind after my father's funeral. The timing of all of this just happens to be a coincidence. I had no idea that they were about to make me partner this soon. I wasn't expecting this for another six months or so."

"Well, you stood in the kitchen and told me that you wanted to wait again until you made Senior Partner."

"I know, but Trent one thing you know about me and that is I would never lie to you. Melina helped me understand the importance of forgiveness and Felicia helped me see what a good man I had. I know how good you are but sometimes it takes seeing things through another person's eyes to make you really realize what you have. When you can step back and see the misfortune of another person it makes you even more appreciative of what you have. Melina also helped me realize that I had a compulsion to over achieve. She helped me to identify the triggers that sparked my compulsion. I had to acknowledge things about myself that I didn't want to admit. For a long time I didn't even think I had a problem. I thought everything was ok; I thought I was ok. I was a fool. I AM a fool, to let you walk out of my life. I love you Trent, more than I could ever love another human being in my life besides my mother. You ARE NOT my Father and I know that you could never hurt me the way my father hurt me. Can you forgive me for holding my father's transgressions against you?"

Kandi got down on one knee and asked Trent, "Trent Bailey, will you marry me?"

"I'm sorry Kandi, it doesn't work that way. Please get up off your knees"

She couldn't believe her ears. She had lost Trent forever. He pulled her off the floor and waited until she was standing. Tears began to roll uncontrollably down her face. She had lost the love of her life. She wasn't going to get a second chance. She had run Trent away for good with her stubbornness. Suddenly all that she had worked so hard for didn't seem worth it at all now.

"Baby, get up off your knees. That's my job", Trent replied as he traded places with Kandi and got down on one knee. "Kandi Johnson, will you marry me?"

"Yes….yes…Trent Bailey I will marry you," Kandi cried out with joy. She knelt down to kiss Trent as he grabbed her in his arms. She held on to him with all of her might. She almost lost the man she loved and she never wanted to let go of him again.

CHAPTER 42

Felicia

Sisterhood - The Culmination

When Felicia opened her eyes all she could see was white all around her. Her first thought was that she had died and gone to heaven because there was so much white. She soon realized that she was in the hospital. This felt like deja vu all over again as she suddenly remembered how she had gotten here. She was just about to close her eyes when she heard a faint knock on the door.
"Come in."

"Hi Felicia, I wanted to come and see how you were doing," said Melina as she stuck her head inside the door. "Are you up for company?"

It was impossible to miss the initial horror in her eyes. Melina did a good job of trying to recover but Felicia had seen her flinch. Felicia could only imagine how horrible she must look. No one else had ever seen her like this before and she couldn't help herself when her eyes became teary.

"Yes, please come in," Felicia replied trying to choke back the tears. Melina was carrying a beautiful floral arrangement. That was so like her; always thinking of others.

"How are you Felicia, really? No secrets this time."

The floodgate of tears opened as Felicia tried to explain to Melina what had happened. "He almost killed me this time Melina. I was so scared. As I was trying to pry his hands from around my neck, it seemed like the harder I fought against him the harder he gripped his hands around my throat. I remember hearing my baby yelling at him to stop and then I must have blacked out because that's the last thing I remember. The next thing I knew I was waking up in here."

"I'm so sorry Felicia."

"He found my certificate hiding in the closet," Felicia explained.

"I never meant for any of this to happen when I suggested you go back to school."

"I know you didn't and this is not your fault. This is not the first time that my husband has beaten me as I am sure you are well aware. It's just been a very long time and I actually thought he was changing. I don't know what to do anymore. I've tried so hard to keep my family together for the sake of my kids."

"Felicia at some point you have to look at the quality of your family and determine what's best for your children. I am in total agreement that the best environment for children is growing up in a household with both parents. I would never advocate a single parent household over a dual parent household when it's a wholesome and nurturing environment. That's why one of the reasons I formed this group was because I know the effects that growing up without a father can have on children but sometimes there are exceptions to the rule. In your situation Felicia this is one of those times. What kind of example is your husband setting for your kids by beating you? He could have killed you. Would you want your son to grow up thinking that it's ok to abuse women? What about your daughters, do you want them to grow up and let men beat them? Physical abuse generally happens in cycles and can become a learned behavior. Yes, your children have a family and a father in the home but it's dysfunctional. Your husband has alienated you from your family so your children have not been able to forge meaningful relationships with their relatives. Your children are not living in an emotionally healthy environment. So in this case, I hate to say it but your children may be better off living apart from their father. I know that it is a contradiction to suggest that you leave your husband but when your physical well-being and safety are in jeopardy than the rules go out the window as far as I am concerned. When you talk to your children be honest with them and tell them the truth. Now I didn't say belittle your husband to them because he is still their father and you have said that he loves his kids. You don't have to go into the details either. Just be truthful with them and hopefully they will grow to understand and respect your decision. You can't protect your children if you're not around anymore."

Melina was right. All the apologies of, "I'm sorry, I won't do it again", and the meaningless confessions of "I love you" had snared Felicia for the last time. She was done listening to Marcus's lies. She was determined not to be a victim anymore. She had to take responsibility of her own situation because as long as she stayed there she allowed Marcus to treat her the way he did. Living in constant fear was no way to live.

She meant every word she said when she told Marcus to kill her. She was sick and tired of living in fear of him. She would rather die than keep living like this and she was never going to let him put his hands on her again or she'd end up killing him. Marcus knew she was serious too because she had actually seen a flicker of fear in his eyes.

238 | SHERRY J. MCFARLAND

If she was ever going to leave him and be happy now was the time to start putting some things in motion. The first thing she had to do was find a job. She would never be able to leave him if she couldn't take care of herself and the kids. Being in the hospital had given Felicia a lot of time to think.

Melina offered to help her in any way she could and Felicia knew she meant it. Sometimes you have to allow other people to help you get out of your situation if you really want to make a change. In fact, Melina was the one who suggested that Felicia go to the women's shelter. Now that Marcus had almost killed her she could have somewhere to go with her children until she got her head together.

Now she only wished that she had told Dr. Anderson the truth so that she could show a pattern of abuse. She had lied to her boss. He thought she had been in an accident so she couldn't use him as a reference. She couldn't use Melina either because when she specifically asked Felicia the truth she had denied it so there was no way she would put Melina in jeopardy by asking her to lie. Felicia had no previous recorded history of Marcus's abuse or anyone to corroborate her story.

She thought about pressing charges but she couldn't. If Marcus was in jail then he couldn't work and then they would be stuck without any insurance or means to pay her hospital bill. She couldn't take food from her kid's mouths by having their father locked away. She didn't make enough money on her part time job to pay all of the bills by herself so she had no choice. She knew everyone would think she was crazy for not pressing charges against him but her kid's needs came first; always.

She did agree to go to a women's shelter when she was released from the hospital. She told Marcus if he ever wanted her to come back home again than he had to give her this time for her body to heal and to get her mind together. Not that he really had a choice, but he agreed to give her the time she needed.

Felicia had really believed that Marcus was changing but this recent blowup changed all that and she realized that he would probably never change. Sometimes it's too little too late and that was the case with her and Marcus.

She decided to move to the west coast and start over. She didn't know anyone there and no one knew her. She had always wanted to move to California and now she finally had the chance to go there. She did a lot of research about going "underground".

Novels, movies and many well-meaning sources have created the fiction of an underground for battered women. The underground supposedly supplies victims with a new identity, transportation to get away, a place to live, a job, money and everything else they need to start a new life. But from what she had been able to find out there really was no such thing as an underground; or at least not the way that it is portrayed.

She did find out, however, that there is an established network of domestic violence shelters. Using the shelter network may be possible but the intake process for a shelter could more than likely require personal information that a person is unwilling to give because it could jeopardize their safety. Some shelters also require that a person file a police report or get an Order of Protection to remain in the shelter. Many women she spoke to had not been aware. Luckily for Felicia she did not have to.

In today's society it has become more unrealistic every day to change your identity as businesses and the government compile enormous shared databases. So it wasn't an easy decision but Felicia decided to leave everything behind. Changing your identity means more than changing your name, social security number, address and phone number. It means you will have to leave behind anything that links to your former identity or that could lead your abuser to you. Changing your identity also has far reaching affects as you will no longer be able to use your work history, credit history, insurance and medical record information, applying for social services, as well as having to conceal your past. It's a daunting task and there are long-lasting consequences of changing your identity but she had to do it.

In retrospect Marcus's obsessive isolation had actually kept Felicia somewhat off the grid of our technological society. He had made it a little easier for her to disappear. She had no credit established in her name other than their house. She would still have to find a way to enroll the kids in school, but she couldn't let that stop her from moving forward with her plans.

Naomi's friend Lance was going to let her and the kids stay in a rental house that he owned in LA. He was letting them stay there for the first year rent free so she could get on her feet. He even offered her a new job in his holding company after he saw the website that she had designed for her own freelance LLC.

Felicia started quietly sneaking her clothes and the kid's clothes out of the house one by one and leaving them in a suitcase that she had packed and stored at Melina's office. The time had finally arrived to go through with the plan she had been devising for the past few months. Everything was ready and there was no turning back now. Too many people had stepped up to help her and she couldn't let them down. As terrified and fearful as she was to leave and face the unknown she was more frightened to stay and face another ten years of misery or even worse; end up dead. She knew that there had to be something out there better for her and her kids and she was determined to find it so she had stashed away four one way tickets in the pocket of a suitcase. They had all been paid for in cash.

One evening Marcus had finally agreed to let the kids spend the night at his sister's house. Felicia had convinced Marcus that they needed some alone; time to start working on their marriage again. She prayed that everything would work out because she hadn't had time to come up with plan B and if she got caught she didn't think she would live through it this time. There was no turning back now; she had to do this.

"Baby they were out of the beer you like the other day when I was at the grocery store".

"Out of beer?"

"Yeah, I guess with the holiday everybody bought up all they had. It will only take me a few minutes to run to the store and get you some more. It should be back in stock by now."

"Ok. Can you bring me back some beef jerky too?"

"Yea, sure. Can you think of anything else?"

"Nah, that's it."

A few minutes later Felicia was backing out the driveway. It had worked! However, instead of driving to the grocery store she drove over to her sister-in-law's house. She tried to remain calm when she walked up to the door. Time was of the essence but she didn't want to raise any suspicion.

Felicia explained to her sister-in-law that Marcus had changed his mind about the kids spending the night and she was there to pick them up. The kids moaned in protest as she gathered their things and scurried them off to the car. She just prayed that her sister-in-law did not call Marcus to fuss at him for changing his mind and not letting the kids spend the night. Paranoia kept Felicia constantly looking in the rearview mirror expecting Marcus to suddenly pop up out of nowhere to stop her.

She drove the car to the bus station. The plan was to ride the bus to Atlanta. From Atlanta they were riding the train to Houston and then catching a plane out to California. Felicia had arranged for Susan to drive the car back to the grocery store and leave it in the parking lot and Melina would pick Susan up from there. By the time Marcus could figure out what was going on they would be well on their way.

Melina, Susan, Kandi and Naomi were all waiting for Felicia and the kids when they pulled into the bus station. Tanisha had already moved out to California so at least now Felicia would know someone out there after all. This was a new adventure for both of them and it would be like having a little sister that she would be able to look out for and vice versa.

Melina had the suitcases that Felicia had been storing in her office. Felicia explained to the kids that they were going away for a while on a little trip. She would explain more to them once they were safely relocated in California. She tried to be strong for her kids but when it came time to board the bus and say goodbye to her friends she couldn't control her emotions anymore.

They hadn't cried together like this since the day Tanisha had the breakthrough in Melina's office. They hugged, they cried and they said their goodbyes. They promised to stay in touch. She loved these women so much. If it wasn't for them Felicia never would have had the courage to change her life forever.

.

CPSIA information can be obtained
at www.ICGtesting.com
Printed in the USA
LVHW010745100721
692198LV00009B/473